"I'm still not sure why you came to me about the pregnancy, Sierra. I'm not sure what you want."

Sierra was afraid to admit what she wanted. She was afraid to admit that making love with Ben Barclay had wiped away everything that had gone before. Had made her lose herself. Had encouraged her to dream again.

"I told you because you had a right to know. If you want to walk away, that's fine. I'll raise this baby on my own."

"That's not going to happen," Ben assured her. "I intend to be a full-fledged father. We'll figure this out, Sierra. It will just take some time."

Figure out how involved they were going to be in each other's lives? Figure out if he wanted to be involved in the pregnancy?

Figure out if one night could have been filled with more than desire?

Dear Reader,

I feel particularly close to my heroine in *The Daddy Verdict.* We share a love of the awe-inspiring New Mexico scenery as well as a kinship for the creative spirit that is so alive there. We also understand that "home" isn't about a place. When Sierra falls in love with Ben, she realizes the bonds between them give her a sense of belonging. She is "home" as long as she's with him. Ben must let his defenses crumble to accept love and discover he has also found "home."

Ben is the third hero in my DADS IN PROGRESS series. I'd love to know which hero—Nathan, Sam or Ben—is your favorite. You can write to me through my Web site at www.karenrosesmith.com, or to P.O. Box 1545, Hanover, PA 17331.

I hope your preparations for the upcoming season bring you "home" for the holidays and always.

All my best,

Karen Rose Smith

THE DADDY VERDICT

KAREN ROSE SMITH

Silhouette®

SPECIAL EDITION®

Published by Silhouette Books

America's Publisher of Contemporary Romance

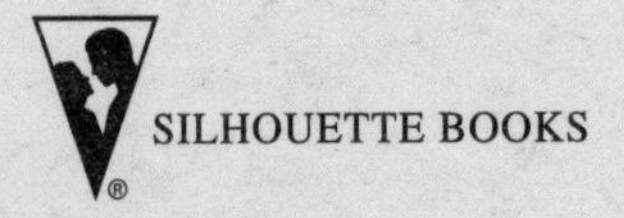

ISBN-13: 978-0-373-24925-1
ISBN-10: 0-373-24925-X

THE DADDY VERDICT

This edition published by arrangement with Harlequin Books S.A.

Visit Silhouette Books at www.eHarlequin.com

Printed in U.S.A.

Books by Karen Rose Smith

Silhouette Special Edition

Abigail and Mistletoe #930
The Sheriff's Proposal #1074
His Little Girl's Laughter #1426
Expecting the CEO's Baby #1535
Their Baby Bond #1588
~*Take a Chance on Me* #1599
Which Child Is Mine? #1655
†*Cabin Fever* #1682
**Custody for Two* #1753
**The Baby Trail* #1767
**Expecting His Brother's Baby* #1779
††*The Super Mom* #1797
‡‡*Falling for the Texas Tycoon* #1807
***The Daddy Dilemma* #1884
°*Her Mr. Right?* #1897
***The Daddy Plan* #1908
***The Daddy Verdict* #1925

~Logan's Legacy
†Montana Mavericks: Gold Rush Grooms
*Baby Bonds
††Talk of the Neighborhood
‡‡Logan's Legacy Revisited
°The Wilder Family
**Dads in Progress

Silhouette Books

The Fortunes of Texas
Marry in Haste...

Logan's Legacy
A Precious Gift

The Fortunes of Texas: Reunion
The Good Doctor

Signature Select

Secret Admirer
"Dream Marriage"

From Here to Maternity
"Promoted to Mom"

KAREN ROSE SMITH

Award-winning and bestselling author Karen Rose Smith has seen more than sixty novels published since 1991. Living in Pennsylvania with her husband—who was her college sweetheart—and their two cats, she has been writing full-time since the start of her career. Lately, in addition to writing, she has been crafting jewelry with her husband. She finds designing necklaces and bracelets relaxing enough to let her mind weave plots while she's beading! Readers can receive updates and excerpts for Karen's latest releases and write to her through her Web site at www.karenrosesmith.com, or send mail to P.O. Box 1545, Hanover, PA 17331.

To my father, Angelo Jacob Cacciola,
who taught me how to build model ships and play blackjack.
I miss you, Daddy.

Chapter One

"I only came here today because…because I'm pregnant." Sierra Girard's blue eyes were wide and vulnerable as her words echoed in Ben Barclay's office.

One thought flashed through his mind—they hadn't used a condom. That oversight had been a first for him.

"Why did you leave without a word?" he asked, feeling as if she'd punched him in the gut with her announcement. Six weeks ago they'd met at a party and had ended up spending the night together…well, most of a night.

Her wavy brown hair fell across her shoulder as she looked down at the purse in her hands, then back up at him. "I left in the middle of the night because we got caught up in the heat of the moment. Because neither of us was looking for what happened. You told me your work was your life…that your job as assistant district attorney took all of your waking hours and many of your sleeping ones."

Pregnant. Sierra was *pregnant!* Ben was suddenly angry at himself and angry with her.

His expression must have shown some of what he was feeling because she murmured, "I never should have come." Turning, she left his office, slipping quickly into the hall.

Instinct made him move like lightning. He grasped her arm.

They both froze, startled once more by the electricity that had drawn them together.

Finally Sierra pulled from his hold. "This isn't your problem. It's mine. I just thought you might like to know."

He and Sierra had started talking at the engagement party of mutual friends. That night her smile had curved around his cynical defenses, breaking down barriers that had been cemented in place for years. Desire had exploded, burning away common sense. After they'd had sex, work exhaustion had caught up to him. He'd fallen asleep…and she'd disappeared.

A colleague walked down the hall and tossed Ben a quizzical look.

"Come back inside," Ben suggested, purposefully keeping his tone calm.

When Sierra hesitated, he added, "You're not going to pull a vanishing act on me again."

"You could have gotten my number from Camille or Miguel if you wanted to reach me," she chided softly.

Had she *wanted* him to search her out?

Why would he want to pursue a woman who'd left without a word or a note? Why would he want to pursue a woman, period? They all left. He knew that too well. His mother had deserted his father, along with him and his two brothers. And after Ben had hit thirty and decided coming home to a woman would be better than returning to an empty apartment, he'd started dating Lois. However, a year and a half later, she'd broken off their relationship because he was too dedicated to his work. She'd been seeing someone else at the public relations firm where she worked *while* he was working! "Love" only had meaning to him in how it related to family. There was no such thing as happily ever after or vows that lasted forever.

Intrigued by Sierra as he had been since they'd met, he asked, "Did you leave that night so I'd chase you?"

"No," she protested so quickly he almost believed her. Then she went on, "I don't tumble into bed with a man every time I go to an engagement party. That night—"

She stopped to gather words that seemed to elude her. "I'd never done anything like that before! I was confused afterward. When you didn't bother to get my number and call, I knew you weren't interested."

Sierra Girard was so beautiful in an innocent, twenty-four-year-old kind of way. He was only thirty-five, but the eleven years' difference seemed more like thirty to him right now. He'd seen things she couldn't imagine in her worst nightmares. The folders on his desk were full of pictures he hoped she'd *never* see.

"Why did you *really* leave the hotel room that night?"

"I thought I was doing the best thing for both of us," she replied with what sounded like sincerity. "That way we didn't have to be embarrassed or awkward, or figure out how to say goodbye."

"Do you always run from awkward situations?" He really didn't know much about her. Just that she and

Camille were good-enough friends for her to be Camille's maid of honor.

At Sierra's pointed silence, Ben raked his hand through his black hair, deciding to let that question go so he could ask something more pertinent. "Have you seen a doctor?"

"Yes, I have."

"What are you going to do about the pregnancy?"

Where before Sierra had seemed almost pale to him, her cheeks took on color now. "I will *not* get an abortion."

"I'm not asking you to consider it." He took a step closer to her, then wished he hadn't because he inhaled her rose-scented perfume. It had driven him crazy at the party the whole time they'd talked, as well as the whole time they'd been naked together. "I just want to know if you can be sure this child is mine."

"It's your baby," she replied quietly. At his silence, she asked, "You don't believe me?"

His poker face must not have been as neutral as he thought. He was short on trust these days, especially where women were concerned, and it must have showed.

"Okay, Ben." Fumbling with the catch on her purse, Sierra reached inside and pulled out a business card. "Here. Now you have my number and the address of my shop. Our baby is due at the end of May. Give me a call if you want to be involved in being a parent. If not, I understand."

Before he could take a breath, Sierra hurried into the hall, her sandals clicking on the tile.

As he watched the sway of her hair across her back, the loose folds of her gauzy dress swinging around her legs, he knew he should call after her…go after her…bring her back to his office until they settled something. But he didn't do any of those things. As one of the most level-headed, steadiest assistant district attorneys in Albuquerque's violent crimes unit, he was shocked to realize he was shaken to his core.

He was going to be a dad!

He had to figure out a plan of action before he talked to Sierra again. He had to figure out if she was sincere, or if she might be trying to use him because she wanted monetary support for a child that might not even be his.

The phone on his desk rang.

Knowing Sierra had probably reached the elevator by now, Ben hurried to pick up the receiver, not at all sure tackling this situation with her would be any easier than prosecuting his hardest case.

Sierra gripped the phone Saturday afternoon as she waited for her aunt's reaction.

"So you told him yesterday and he said…" Gina Ruiz prompted her niece from across the globe.

Sierra paced back and forth behind the counter of her shop, Beaded for You, on the outskirts of Old Town, Albuquerque. Her aunt Gina was questioning her with the fierce protectiveness of a mother. Her aunt had been more of a parent than either of her parents ever had, and Sierra loved her for it.

"He was…shocked."

"I suppose that's good. That means something like this doesn't happen to him every day."

In spite of Sierra's queasy stomach, which always seemed to become unsettled midafternoon, she had to smile. "I should hope not. I never would have ended up in bed with him if I'd thought—"

She stopped, realizing what she had just said. This was her aunt, for goodness sake, not Camille.

"What happened, Sierra? This kind of thing isn't like you at all. You told me Ben Barclay is going to be Miguel's best man, but you don't really know him, do you? Did he take advantage of you in some way? Put something in your drink? Did you have too many glasses of wine to celebrate Camille and Miguel's engagement?"

Sierra remembered her first glimpse of Ben at the party. Oh, he was handsome all right, with black hair, thick brows, defined cheekbones and a jaw that looked very stern, except when he smiled. When his gray eyes had held hers for a long moment across the room, she'd felt… breathless, and had been unsettled by the tingles that had danced down her spine. With good reason. She didn't date because the memories of her fiancé and the selflessness that had gotten him killed were still too fresh at times.

But, as Sierra knew, fate wasn't something you could control. After she and Ben had been introduced, they'd begun a conversation about his work, about her shop. The room had gotten very noisy. She'd sensed he liked quiet as much as she did when he'd invited her to his room. She'd never expected their conversation would lead to bed.

"Sierra?"

"Aunt Gina, he was the perfect gentleman. I mean, it was both of us. It just happened. I'm not sure why or how. It just did."

"Do you want me to come home?"

Sierra's mother and father were anthropologists who traveled the world. Although they'd kept her with them when she was small, she'd always known she was secondary to whatever they shared, including their work. Her mother found nannies and teachers for her and often brought her back to New Mexico to spend weeks or months with her aunt.

Sierra had always felt extraneous. Once on a visit home, she'd heard her parents arguing with her aunt, her mother's sister, about her need for *normal* high school years, a chance to socialize with children her own age and make bonds that would last longer than six months or a year. When Aunt Gina had invited Sierra to live with her for her four years of high school, Sierra had accepted joyfully, and would always be filled with gratitude for that time of her life.

Now her aunt was in Greece, a trip she had planned for most of her adult life. Sierra wasn't going to make her cut it short.

"There's no need for you to come home. Honestly, I'm fine. I really am. Camille and Miguel are here and so are other friends. I'll be busy with Camille's wedding next weekend."

"But who will look after you when they're away? What if you have a problem?"

"I can look after myself. My doctor's a phone call away. Honestly, Aunt Gina, please don't worry."

The security bell dinged as her shop door opened. Ben Barclay walked in!

"Aunt Gina, Ben just came in. I have to go."

"Don't let him make decisions for you," her aunt warned.

"I won't."

"Call me again soon."

"I will. I love you," she murmured into the cell phone, and after her aunt returned the sentiment, Sierra closed it.

With the brilliant New Mexico sun behind Ben, he stood in shadow until he approached the counter. His gaze assessed the space quickly—the glass cases filled with beaded jewelry created of lapis and tiger eye, turquoise and Venetian glass. She couldn't tell from his expression what he thought, but she'd already learned that was normal for an encounter with Ben. Dressed in black cargo pants and a rust-and-black Henley shirt, he looked every bit as handsome as he had in his suit. She couldn't keep other pictures from clicking through her mind—broad bare shoulders, curling black chest hair, powerful muscles….

Sierra warned herself not to expect anything from him. There was an edge to him that she suspected came from his work—all-encompassing work, like her fiancé's had been. Travis had been a doctor, and his vocation had been to save lives. Ben saved lives, too, in a different way. He put the bad guys away so they couldn't hurt anyone again. But his work had been another reason she'd left his room so quickly that night. Right or wrong, dedicated men didn't put the people they loved first.

Ben approached the sales counter where she stood. "At the party you told me you make jewelry. Which are yours?" He was obviously starting with soft conversation before they delved into the tough stuff.

"I made all of it. At least when I get insomnia, I have something to do," she joked, though it was hard to come up with a smile, wondering why he'd come and what he would say.

Ben's gray eyes took in everything about her, from her turquoise blouse to her brown gaucho pants. They came back to rest on her necklace, the long dangle of beads that rested between the plackets of her blouse. "Did you make that?"

His gaze on her melted her insides as she nodded. When he'd made love to her, nothing had existed except the two of them.

His thumb ran over a turquoise nugget, then the round coral beads beneath it. "You're a talented woman."

"I just have a knack for putting together colors and shapes."

Dropping the dangle as if it were suddenly too hot to handle, he said, "I want to be part of my baby's life…if this child *is* my baby."

In some ways she knew life would be easier and less complicated if she parented their child alone. Still, she answered, "It is."

He scrutinized her for a long moment. "We'll have a DNA test done after the baby's born. But until then, I want to know what's happening. Do you need financial assistance?"

His jaw had set after he asked the question, and Sierra wondered if he believed she was just after money. "I don't need help."

"Do you have insurance?"

"Yes, I do. I didn't come to you because I wanted anything."

"You just thought I should know?"

The repetition of her reasoning sounded lame when he said it, but it *was* the truth. "I have an appointment with my obstetrician Thursday after next. If you're interested in meeting her, if you have questions…"

She trailed off, feeling they were moving toward an intimacy she wasn't ready for. And it had nothing to do with having sex. The intimacy involved becoming parents together.

"I have a trial coming up, but if there's any way I can be at your appointment, I will. Just let me know when and where."

This was so awkward. She'd never dated much. By the time she'd gone to public high school, the other girls were way ahead of her with their flirting skills. She'd always just wanted to meet someone who would understand her... whom she could understand. Travis had been the one. Even though her aunt had told her she was too young to get seriously involved at twenty, her parents, on the other hand, had told her to follow her heart. She had.

"What are you thinking about?" Ben asked, and she realized memories must have shone in her eyes.

"I was thinking about what brought me here."

"To Albuquerque?"

"No, not exactly. To age twenty-four, having the shop, meeting you and now getting pregnant."

He waited for a moment as if to see if she'd say more. But she didn't. She didn't know him well enough. She'd been so foolish to let unexpected desire lead her here.

"You said you live with your aunt. Do you have other family in Albuquerque?"

She shook her head. "No. My parents are in Africa right now. And even my aunt—" She stopped, not knowing how many personal details she wanted to give him.

"Your aunt?"

"She's traveling. She'll be back in a few weeks."

"Does she know about the pregnancy?"

"I called her this afternoon. I wanted to tell you first."

That seemed to give him pause. "How about Camille?"

"If we have any alone time before the wedding, I'll

tell her. But if not, I'll wait until she returns from her honeymoon."

"Are you planning to stay overnight at the hacienda after the wedding?"

Miguel Padilla's parents lived in a hacienda outside of Santa Fe. That's where the wedding was going to be held, though the reception would be celebrated at the inn where Sierra and Ben had attended the engagement party. "I'll be staying over. Camille's mother wants to talk to me about Christmas presents she'd like me to make for her nieces. What about you?"

"I hadn't decided yet, but now I'm beginning to think it might be a good idea. In fact, we could go together."

That suggestion urged her to take a deep breath. "Together?"

"We're going to have decisions to make. Don't you think it would be a good idea if we got to know each other?"

Sierra really hadn't thought past telling Ben the news about the pregnancy, simply because she hadn't known what his reaction would be...or how he'd feel about fatherhood. Maybe the weekend would provide them with a good opportunity to figure out whether or not they *could* parent together.

When she didn't answer right away, he frowned. "Look, if that's too complicated—"

"No. No, it's not. I just...I hadn't thought past telling you I was pregnant. I thought you'd want nothing to do with me and the baby."

"How did you get that impression?"

"Your career takes up most of your time. Besides, this isn't the kind of responsibility a man takes on willingly."

"You assumed I wouldn't be willing."

"I suppose I did."

The silence floated around them like the dust motes in the sunlight. Finally, Ben concluded, "Maybe after next weekend we'll both know each other better."

There was something about Ben that drew Sierra toward him. It also made her a little afraid. Not physically afraid or anything like that…just afraid because he looked at her with so many questions, as if she wasn't telling him the truth. He looked at her as if she were on one side of the fence and he was on the other. Maybe her imagination was just going wild and he wasn't as complicated as she thought he was.

Just as she'd done in *his* office, he took a card from his pocket and handed it to her. "My cell phone number's on there. You can always reach me. I'll give you a call later in the week and we'll set up a time for Saturday."

She nodded. As he turned to leave, she called his name. "Ben?"

He faced her once more.

"Thanks for making this a little easier."

"We'll see how easy it is once we get deeper into it." Then he left her shop.

Had she made a mistake agreeing to go to the wedding with him? She could back out, tell him she wanted to drive herself.

But that would be the cowardly thing to do. She *wasn't* a coward.

Chapter Two

"Are you ready?" Ben asked in that way he had of appraising Sierra that made her feel turned inside out.

Flustered and nervous after opening her door to him, she asked herself for the umpteenth time why she'd agreed to drive with him to Santa Fe for Camille and Miguel's wedding. "Sure am. I just have to grab my duffel bag and gown. Come on in."

Friendly. She'd just be friendly and polite and keep her distance. But that was difficult when excitement tingled through her from studying him in his black polo shirt and khaki slacks.

She stood aside to let him in.

As soon as he stepped into the casita's small living room, she realized just how hard keeping her distance would be. Tall, fit and broad-shouldered, Ben seemed to take up the entire room.

"This is nice," he remarked, assessing the space. A tan ceramic-tiled counter separated the appliances from a table for four and a hutch displaying artifacts. The house had an alarm to protect them and other treasures her aunt had gathered over the years.

"It's been my home as much as any place has," Sierra admitted.

"You said you lived with your aunt when you attended high school."

Apparently he'd listened and remembered. "Yes, and since I returned to Albuquerque a few years ago." She went to the sofa to pick up her garment bag.

"You didn't say much about where you lived before returning here."

Avoiding his gaze, she lifted her duffel. "We can talk about that in the car if you want to get going."

Before she could guess what he was going to do, his hand reached out for her bag. "I'll take that."

"I'm stronger than I look," she joked.

He stood very close, so close she could catch the scent of his aftershave. "I imagine you are. But if you want to lock the door, you'll need a free hand."

He was right *and* one step ahead of her.

Somehow in passing the duffel's strap to him, their hands brushed. His skin was hot, slightly rough. She remembered exactly how his hands had felt on her skin.

When their gazes collided, neither of them breathed for a moment. But then Ben motioned to the door. "Ladies first." His expression was unreadable as she set the alarm, then stepped outside.

After he stowed her duffel on the floor in the backseat of his SUV, he hung her gown across from his tuxedo.

Sierra had already fastened her seat belt when he climbed in. He stared at her for a few seconds and didn't start the ignition.

"What?" she asked.

"I'm surprised you don't have more luggage."

"We're just going overnight."

"Yeah, but with the wedding and all…"

What had he expected? A huge cosmetics case, a suitcase filled with alternate outfits? "I'm a traveler, remember? I've learned to pack light."

"You're one of the few women on earth who can do that." He turned the key.

"Actually, my mother is another. That's one handy trait she taught me."

After he pulled out onto the street, he drove to the intersection. But at the stoplight, he glanced at her again. "You said your parents were anthropologists and you traveled with them until you came back here to live with your aunt while you were in high school."

"That's right."

"You were an only child?"

"I was."

"Then why did they let you return here to live during your most formative years? Why didn't they want to see you go out on your first date, drive your first car, attend a prom?"

Ben might have an edge sometimes—she'd sensed a cynicism about him from the moment she'd met him—but he was much too perceptive, too. Had that talent come from perfecting interrogation skills? Or from trying to read witnesses and criminals?

"My parents are a little unusual."

"How so?" He turned onto a main street and headed for I-25.

In the past she'd never let anyone but her aunt see how her childhood years had affected her, how lonely she'd been, how the feeling of not being wanted superseded all others. Now that she'd set foot in this conversation, she didn't know quite how to step out of it.

Sticking to the basics, she explained, "My parents were totally engrossed in their careers."

"Lots of parents are," he remarked.

"I suppose so."

Ben wasn't going to let that be the end of it. "So how did their preoccupation with their careers affect you?"

"Are you trying to psychoanalyze me?"

Again he tossed her a quick look. "No, just trying to understand your background."

"Are you going to tell me about yours? I mean, I know you're from Minnesota, but that's about it."

"Are you evading my question?"

She had to remember she was dealing with a lawyer, a man who was used to getting answers. She had the feeling he wouldn't give up until he did.

After another few moments of hesitation, she agreed, "Yes, lots of parents are engrossed in their careers. That's true. But to explain my parents' lives..." She hesitated again.

He waited, expecting her to go on.

She *could* just clam up, but if they were in this for the long haul, she should give him a hint of what her childhood had been. "You told me your work is demanding and you're busy even nights and weekends."

"I did."

"Well, imagine this. Imagine that you married another A.D.A. whose dedication and work ethic was the same as yours. On top of that, imagine that you worked with her on every case, all day, every day. Then picture your wife having a baby and the two of you still wanting to work every case together and wanting to go back to the way things were before the baby was born."

He went silent for at least a half mile until they veered off the main road onto the interstate and headed for Santa Fe. Finally, he offered, "If I imagined that scenario, then I'd also imagine a nanny raising the baby, right?"

"Mom and Dad were researchers, so I had lots of nannies." Usually native women whom she'd come to love and respect. But she'd felt so separated from her mom and dad as they'd interviewed villagers, discussed their theories, written up their findings.

Ben's mouth tightened. "Where were you born?"

"In France. My father was French and his mother was living then. From the accounts I've heard, my parents went there in my mom's ninth month and we stayed for three months after I was born."

"And then?"

"Then they went to Africa, then Bali, India and South America."

"How many languages do you speak?"

"A few."

"I'll bet! So what happens in a child's head when she settles in and then has to move again—someplace strange and foreign where she doesn't even know the language—and her parents are preoccupied with their careers?"

No matter how she'd tried to be factual and not emotional, Ben had focused on the undercurrent. "I lived in books if I had access to them. When I didn't, I learned the crafts of the people we lived with."

"Crafts. You mean like cooking, making clay pots?"

"Basket making, weaving, dying yarn, etching, whittling. You name it, I've probably done it." Definitely wanting to change the topic, she asked, "Are you close to your family?"

"'Close' is a relative term, but yes, I think I am. We call one another when we need something. I go home for holidays when I can."

"The night of Camille and Miguel's engagement party, you mentioned your dad and going ice fishing with him. What about your mom?"

The silence that invaded the car at Sierra's question told her more than any words could that Ben's childhood hadn't been perfection, either. "She left when I was six."

"Left your dad?"

"Left my dad, Nathan, Sam, me and Rapid Creek."

She could tell this wasn't territory Ben traveled often, either. To push or not to push. If she knew more about his background, she might understand him better, right?

"Where did she go?"

"It's not important. She just went. Dad wiped her out of our lives. He finally told us she'd died when Nathan went to college."

"And you didn't know?" Sierra was absolutely shocked.

"When she left, she didn't stay in touch."

Although Ben was obviously trying to keep his tone neutral, she heard bitterness and she stopped asking questions. They'd both shared enough for one session.

It was so much easier to concentrate on the scenery she

loved. New Mexico was absolutely her favorite place on earth. No sky seemed as blue, no clouds seemed as close, no cliffs seemed quite as awe-inspiring. From the Sandia Mountains northeast of Albuquerque to the Sangre de Cristos east of Santa Fe, from the piñon pines along the Rio Grande to the sage, coyote fences and adobes, New Mexico made her feel as if she fit here in a way she didn't fit anywhere else. Maybe it was because her aunt lived here and her aunt had been the one loving, guiding, gentle force for her whole life. Yet her aunt wasn't the only reason. There was something about the creative spirit here that just enveloped Sierra in loving arms.

Obviously also wanting to end their conversation for now, Ben switched on the CD player. Strings of an acoustic guitar and flute floated into the car. It was the kind of music she liked, too. Did she and Ben have common interests?

She doubted it more and more as the miles passed and he didn't speak. He seemed to be miles away, and she suspected he wasn't thinking about the wedding.

Sierra left Ben to his thoughts for the remainder of the drive. She refused to think beyond today. She was going to enjoy her best friend's wedding and try to find out more about Ben. But something told her finding out more about him might lead her someplace she didn't want to go. With him beside her in the car, it was hard to escape memories of the night they'd shared. But for now, she had to put them aside. She had to think clearly. She couldn't let the sight of his strong hands on the steering wheel remind her of how those hands had made her feel.

She was almost relieved when they took the road to the Padilla family's hacienda. The black, wrought-iron gates were open, welcoming them. A sprawling peach adobe house nestled against the hills while a tiered fountain in the front courtyard bubbled and streamed.

They'd almost reached the protective arch above the door when the heavy oak portal opened and Camille came running out. She embraced Sierra and then saw Ben holding Sierra's gown and duffel. "What's this? Did you two come together?"

Before Sierra could answer, Ben replied, "It seemed the practical thing to do."

"Why, yes, I guess it *would* be practical," Camille agreed, her dark eyes sparkling with curiosity as she arched a brow at Sierra, and her black hair blew in the fall breeze.

As they all stepped inside the foyer, Ben said, "I can just drop this all in Sierra's room. Which one is hers?"

"Upstairs, second door on the right."

After Ben headed that way, Camille looked at her friend. "What haven't you told me?"

Sierra felt her cheeks warm. "We'll have to talk when you have some time."

"I'll make the time," Camille assured her.

"Sure, you will. In between saying your vows, dancing your wedding dance and leaving for your honeymoon."

"Sierra, how nice to see you again!" Camille's mother, Maria, greeted her as she joined them. "You look beautiful, as always. But I'm going to have to steal my daughter away now. It's time for her to get dressed."

"Mom, I have plenty of time."

"Not as much as you think. Sierra, once you're dressed, come down to the master suite. That's where Camille will be. Mrs. Padilla and I will be helping her get ready there."

Camille rolled her eyes and murmured to Sierra, "This is a tradition of some kind."

"Traditions are good," Sierra tossed back with a smile, knowing she was going to begin lots of traditions for the child she carried…so many her son or daughter wouldn't be able to count them all.

She gave Camille a hug. "Go on. Make yourself beautiful for your husband-to-be. I'll see you in a little while."

As Sierra wound her way through the living room to the stairway that led to the second floor, she found Ben just mounting the steps.

"I got waylaid by Miguel—last-minute instructions," he explained.

"Anything I should know about?"

"I don't think so. Apparently there was a glitch and the wedding arch just arrived. But it's set up now and all the chairs are in place. He said there are enough flowers to open his own shop."

Sierra laughed. "Camille loves flowers, especially jasmine and gardenias."

"That's what's there."

As they walked up the beautiful oak stairs, the scent of lemon oil permeated the space. Ben asked, "What's your favorite flower?"

She looked over her shoulder at him. "I'm partial to roses, especially pale pink ones."

"You wear the scent of roses." He reached the landing a step behind her.

"You noticed!"

Beside her now on the second floor, he gazed into her eyes and admitted, "I noticed a lot about you, Sierra. That's how we ended up in bed together."

Her cheeks began to burn. Apparently Ben said exactly what was on his mind. She turned toward the second door on the right.

After she stepped over the threshold into the guest room, she appreciated the white iron bedstead, carved oak furniture, beautiful lace curtains and colorful rugs on the floor.

Ben lifted the dress. "Where do you want this?"

She took it from him, opened the closet and hung it inside. "I might have to touch it up with an iron."

He carried her duffel bag to the bed and set it on the mattress. His gaze lingered on the bed and hers did, too.

They looked up at the same time and their eyes locked.

As if she'd stepped into a time machine, Sierra was tossed back seven weeks. The room was Ben's room at the inn, the bed was Ben's bed. They'd sat on the edge of it, talking, and then the talking had turned into kissing.

They'd undressed each other hungrily. They'd come together so passionately, thought had fled. Good sense had gotten buried and only desire had mattered. Although they'd been eager, Ben hadn't rushed with her. He'd made sure she was as hot and needy as he was. And when he'd entered her, he'd blotted out the rest of the world.

But then she'd awakened, knowing he'd have regrets and so would she. So she'd left.

Not removing his gaze from hers, Ben approached her slowly.

Her mouth suddenly seemed very dry.

"When you left in the middle of the night, you knew we'd see each other again today."

"Yes, I did."

"How were you going to play that? How were you going to act?"

"If you hadn't contacted me, I would have pretended that night never happened. How about you?"

"I don't think I could have pretended it never happened. I would have asked you why you didn't stay."

"It was a mistake."

"You decided that for *me,* too?" There was a hard edge to his voice, as if he didn't like that idea at all.

"If it hadn't been a mistake, you would have called."

"Women," Ben said, shaking his head. "*You* left, but *I* was supposed to call?"

"It really doesn't matter anymore, does it?"

"I think maybe it does. I want to know the real reason why you left. The truth, Sierra. Not just something you think I might want to hear."

Could she tell him the truth? His turbulent gray eyes told her that she'd better or he'd never believe another thing she said. She swallowed hard. "You scared me."

That completely shocked him. "Did I hurt you in some way?"

"No," she quickly replied. "No, you didn't hurt me. I guess I said that wrong. *You* didn't scare me. Your intensity scared me because I responded to it. I…that was the first time for me in a long time. I didn't think I was ready. I didn't think I could—I'm not putting this very well. It was just very unnerving for me. I didn't know how to deal with it so I left."

His gray gaze was penetrating, as if he wanted to turn her inside out…see to the very bottom of her soul. Finally he admitted, "I don't trust easily, Sierra. I'm still not sure why you came to me about the pregnancy. I'm still not sure what you want."

She was afraid to admit what she wanted. She was

afraid to admit that making love with Ben Barclay had wiped away everything that had gone before, had made her lose herself, had encouraged her to dream again.

Although she wanted to turn away, lessen the strong vibrations that shook her when she was around him, she looked right into his eyes. "I meant it when I said I don't want anything from you. I told you because you had a right to know. What you want to do about it is your choice. If you want to walk away after today, that's fine. I'll raise this baby on my own."

"That's not going to happen," he assured her. "Once I know this baby's mine, I intend to be a full-fledged father."

"You still don't believe me?"

When he didn't reply, she knew the answer. He'd just told her he didn't trust easily and that was absolutely the truth.

Reaching out, he grazed her cheek with the back of his hand. "We'll figure this out, Sierra. It will just take some time."

Figure out how involved they were going to be in each other's lives? Figure out if he wanted to be involved in the pregnancy? Figure out if one night could have been filled with more than desire? The reasons why she'd left that night still held. She didn't know if she was ready for another intimate relationship, especially with a man like Ben, a man dedicated to a career that was all-important to him. She had to remember *that* before she took another step toward him, before she let him take a step toward her.

She backed away. "I'd better get ready."

He nodded. "My tuxedo's still in the car." He crossed to the door. "I'll see you at the wedding."

When Ben closed the door behind him, Sierra sank

onto the bed. All she had to do was think about Camille and Miguel and the next few hours would be easy.

If she said that often enough, she *might* believe it.

Ben shrugged into his tuxedo jacket, then checked his pocket for the wedding ring. He heard the floorboards creak in the room next door. Was Sierra styling her hair? Applying makeup? Slipping into her gown? All too easily he could recall exactly what she'd looked like naked and become aroused by the picture.

Damn! How could she possibly be as innocent as she looked? Was he really supposed to believe she wanted nothing from him?

He thought of his mother leaving his father all those years ago, and his father's bitterness and unhappiness after she left. His brothers' sadness. His own feeling that he'd done something wrong to make her leave. Weren't mothers supposed to love their children no matter what?

He heard the water running in Sierra's bathroom, then it was quickly shut off. He could picture her applying lipstick to her full lips or brushing her luxurious hair.

Intentionally, he thought about Lois, the woman he'd thought he'd marry some day. She'd been beautiful in a much more sophisticated way than Sierra. She'd been a professional woman, serious about her career in public relations. He'd thought she'd understand working early, working late, working weekends. Before she'd left, before she'd told him she'd already found someone else, she'd said something he hadn't been able to forget. "I still feel alone, even when I'm in the same room with you, Ben."

He wasn't sure exactly what that had meant.

Instead of focusing on a past that couldn't be changed

or Sierra, who unsettled him more than he wanted to admit, he turned his attention to another situation that had preoccupied his thoughts.

Last night after a basketball workout with the teenagers he'd befriended, he'd approached his car in the public parking lot. The hairs on the back of his neck had twitched. He always paid attention to that feeling. Although years before he'd earned a black belt in karate, his skills had gotten rusty with disuse. Last night he'd reached into his jeans pocket for his pocketknife, flipped it open and kept his hand by his side. Then he'd heard, "Hey, Mr. District Attorney."

A man had suddenly appeared from behind a truck. Although he'd been of average height with lank brown hair and a too-large black shirt hanging over worn jeans, a memory had flickered in Ben's brain.

"I have fifty dollars in cash and one credit card," Ben had said reasonably, his thumb securing a firm place on the knife handle.

"I don't want your money," the man had declared. "I want you to lay off my brother. He's innocent."

"Who's your brother?" Ben had asked to gain time.

"Charlie Levsin. If you don't back off, something could happen to you."

Ben had considered the death threat he'd received in August. It had come in with his mail in a plain white envelope, one sheet of paper printed on a computer. *You are going to die.* Although he'd received death threats before, this time his boss had suggested he leave town for a few days and he had, to help his brother Sam lay floors in his new house. There had been nothing since then.

Levsin's trial was scheduled for December. Ben had

known better than to alienate Levsin's brother. "Threatening my life could get you in trouble."

"There ain't nobody here to hear me. Your word against mine. Just make sure my brother gets off."

Ben had evidence up the kazoo against Levsin and there was no way he was going to back down. "The jury will decide whether he's innocent or guilty."

"Yeah, well, they'd better decide he's innocent. I mean it, Mr. D.A. You throw that trial or you'll be sorry."

As quickly as the man had appeared, he'd disappeared.

If Ben had chased him, caught him and hauled him in, they could have held him for a while. But it would have just been his word against Ben's.

Ben's thoughts were interrupted when his phone rang. Plucking it from the dresser, he opened it. When he checked the caller ID, he was relieved to see his brother Nathan's number.

"You almost caught me at the altar," Ben joked, pushing away the sound of Levsin's voice that had played in his head since last night.

It took Nathan a moment to absorb what Ben had said, then he replied, "Sorry. I forgot you were a best man again this weekend."

"It's okay. I have a few minutes. I was just checking to make sure I had Miguel's ring for Camille in my pocket."

"I remember when you handed me the ring for Sara."

"No regrets?" Ben asked, really curious.

"Not a one. I'm a lucky man. Who would have thought I'd find another woman who could put up with me?"

Ben laughed. "I think Sara does more than put up with you."

"You've come to accept her."

"Yeah, almost like a sister. She's a straight talker and you know I appreciate that."

"What about Corrie? Sam mentioned he thought the two of you got along really well when you flew home to help us lay floors in his new house."

His brother Sam was a newlywed, too. "I like Corrie. She's not quite as open and free as Sara, but anyone who loves animals like Sam does has a good heart. She's pretty honest about what she thinks, too."

"Women these days are like that."

Ben thought about Sierra…their news. He didn't keep secrets from his brothers. Well, that wasn't completely true. He hadn't told them about the death threat. He wouldn't, either. Yet that was different. "My life got a little more complicated recently."

"Work?" Nathan asked.

"Not this time. I…uh…" He suddenly felt tongue-tied. "I found out I'm going to be a father."

The silence told Ben that Nathan was thinking how best to respond. Finally his brother asked, "Are congratulations in order?"

"You mean, am I happy about it? I'm still trying to get used to the idea. But the more I think about it, yeah, I think I'm happy about it. You know how I love spending time with Kyle." His nephew was one of his favorite people.

"So you're involved with someone?"

"Not exactly."

"You'd better explain that."

Ben blew out a sigh. He had to admit his stupidity to his brother. "I messed up. First time ever. Remember the engagement party I told you about?"

"The one in Santa Fe, where Miguel asked you to be best man."

"Yeah. Well, Camille's maid of honor and I started talking. One thing led to another, and she's pregnant."

"You've been dating her since the party? You didn't say a word."

"No, I haven't been dating her. After that night, she left. I just figured it was a night she didn't want to repeat. But she turned up at my office to give me the news."

"So she's there with you this weekend?"

"We decided to come together. I mean, we drove together. We're here separately. Nothing's going to happen."

Nathan was quiet, then replied wryly, "Something already did. You advised both me and Sam to be careful about custody issues. Is it going to be a problem for you?"

"I don't know yet. I don't know Sierra that well. That's partially why I suggested we come together this weekend."

"Does she want the baby?"

"She seems to and said she wouldn't consider an abortion."

"You know a good custody lawyer?"

"Sure do. I hope it's not going to come to that. Sierra hasn't had roots. Her parents are anthropologists and move around a lot. On one hand, she could just take off and join them anytime. On the other hand, her aunt's here and so is her shop. Sara would love the handmade jewelry."

"Maybe Sara will get a chance to see it. That's actually why I called. How would you like some company for Thanksgiving?"

"What brought this on?"

"Well, you know Sara and I have applied to adopt. Something could come through at any time. Once we have another child, traveling could be more difficult. Kyle wants to see those petroglyphs you tell him about whenever you visit. So we thought this might be a good time to take a trip. How do you feel about that?"

"I'm swamped at work and I didn't know if I could fly out for Thanksgiving. So, yeah, it would be great. Dad won't mind?"

"Nah. He and Val will spend it with Sam and Corrie and her dad. By Thanksgiving, there will hopefully be a baby to hold."

Corrie's due date was November 11. But with a first baby, Ben knew anything could happen. "If you fly out for Thanksgiving, you can give me your opinion of Sierra."

"Does my opinion matter?"

"Sure it does. I checked out Sara before you got involved."

"Yes, I guess you did."

"I haven't figured out Sierra yet. She says she doesn't want anything from me. She says she can raise this child alone. But that's not going to happen."

"Just be careful, Ben, especially if you want to be a dad."

"I'll be careful. Remember, I know the ins and outs of the law."

A few minutes later after Ben said goodbye to his brother, he pocketed his phone. Then he went downstairs to find Miguel, eager to see Sierra walk down the aisle. Weddings seemed to bring out both the best and the worst in people since they were highly emotionally charged events. He'd be watching Sierra carefully throughout the day, to see if she was the sincere woman she seemed to be. Actions always spoke louder than words.

Then he would decide exactly what he was going to do about the custody issue.

Chapter Three

Ben felt poleaxed as Sierra walked down the aisle toward him. He stood beside Miguel to the left side of the arch waiting for the main event—the bride marching down the aisle with her father. But first, her maid of honor prepared the way.

Sierra's gown had been encased in a garment bag so he'd had no idea what it would look like. He'd never quite expected this. The turquoise fabric was filmy and floaty. The expression on her face got to him. She was thoroughly happy for her friends. He caught the sheen of tears in her eyes as she gripped her bouquet tighter.

They hadn't rehearsed since only two of them were in the wedding party, but Miguel had told Ben what to do. He walked to the center of the aisle to meet Sierra and let her hook her arm into his as he escorted her to the right side of the arch. She held on to him as if the moment might be too emotion-filled for her to handle alone. But then she released him, stepped away, independent and so very beautiful. He could only stare at her for a moment before he once more took his place beside Miguel.

Tearing his attention from Sierra, he heard the swell of music created by the guitars and violins located to the side of the guests, then focused on the bride as she walked up the aisle.

He tapped Miguel's shoulder. "You're a lucky man."

But as Miguel murmured, "I know," and stepped to meet his bride in the middle of the aisle, Ben's gaze fell again on Sierra. Their eyes locked and held, but then she looked away to watch Camille's father hand his daughter to her future husband.

The minister motioned them forward and the ceremony began.

The ceremony, however, didn't make an impact as Camille handed her bouquet to Sierra, as the couple bowed their heads in prayer, as they exchanged vows and then rings. Ben's mind whirred with future pictures of Sierra as a mother with a newborn in her arms, rocking the baby to sleep, feeding the son or daughter that was a part of him.

But *was* this baby part of him? *Was* this child his? He didn't know Sierra. He didn't know her morals. He didn't know if she slept around. Only a DNA test would tell him the truth. Women lied, he knew that. Hadn't his father told him from his teenage years on that women were selfish, that they did what was best for *them,* not what was best for their family? His mother had proven that to all of them. Lois, instead of telling him what she wanted and needed, had turned to another man.

He didn't want to accept the fact that he was an expectant father, only later to be disappointed. Better to stay removed than to care. Better to learn the truth now than later. In his job, he had to constantly separate the truth from lies. He was practiced at discerning the truth and he'd do exactly that with Sierra.

"We're supposed to mingle," Ben murmured close to Sierra's ear as he stood behind her to pull out her chair.

The reception was being held in the same room at the Inn where Camille had introduced Sierra to Ben. Throughout dinner she'd sat beside Camille at the head table while Ben was positioned on the other side next to Miguel. Even so, she was aware of him in a way she'd never been aware of another man—not even Travis. She wasn't sure how she felt about *that.*

As Sierra stood and rounded the table, Ben's hand rested protectively at the small of her back. The heat of it easily penetrated the chiffon.

They were headed for the table where the bride and groom's parents sat when a little girl of about five, who was dressed in a pretty pink taffeta dress, chased a boy who must have been her younger brother. The boy dashed around Sierra, but the little girl ran right into her.

"Whoa!" Sierra caught her, steadying them both. She felt Ben's strong hands steady *her.*

The girl looked up at Sierra with fearful wide blue eyes, as if she was preparing herself to be scolded.

Sierra just smiled. "Do you think you could slow down a little? If you slip in those pretty shoes, you might fall and get hurt."

The child poked her finger into her mouth and tentatively smiled back, mumbling, "Okay."

"What's your name?" Sierra asked.

"Trisha."

"Trisha, you look almost as pretty as the bride today. Were you chasing your brother?"

Trisha nodded again. "He wants to play tag."

"Maybe you could tell him tag would be a better game *out*side."

Trisha pointed to the table where the boy had run. A woman who looked to be in her thirties was gesturing to the chair beside her. "Mommy's probably telling him that."

"Probably," Sierra agreed.

"I'll tell Mommy you said I'm as pretty as Camille." Trisha quickly walked toward her mom, looking back at Sierra and waving.

Sierra waved back.

Ben tilted his head and studied her. "Have you had much experience with kids?"

"I was one," she teased.

He rolled his eyes. "You know what I mean. You don't have brothers or sisters. You weren't around family growing up."

"No, but I did make friends wherever we went. There were two ways to handle each situation when we moved. I could either be on my own so that when we left again, leaving friends behind wouldn't hurt, or I could just jump right in and get involved, make friends and hope someday we'd see each other again. I jumped in. I didn't like being lonely."

Ben looked thoughtful. "Did you see any of your friends again after you moved away?"

"Unfortunately, no. But it was the hope of seeing them

again that mattered, and I have a lot of years left to still do it. Who knows? I might return to Brazil or Africa."

The violinist and guitar players, instead of just playing background music, had launched into a rendition of "Endless Love," one of Camille's favorite songs. She and Miguel moved to the middle of the dance floor, ready for their first dance as newlyweds. They looked so happy.

"Next dance we're going to have to go out there," Ben reminded her.

The second dance would also be for the parents, Ben and Sierra and any of the guests who wanted to join in. The idea of being held in Ben's arms again sent a tremble up her spine.

When the love song ended, the instrumentalists began an up-to-date slow melody.

Ben motioned to the dance floor. "Ready?"

She was as ready as she was going to be. She nodded.

He didn't touch her—she could still recall too vividly the feel of his fingers on her cheek—until they reached the dance floor. He didn't hesitate then, just opened his arms in the usual ballroom position. She took his hand and laid her arm on his shoulder. His arm went around her and rested lightly on her waist. The room around her with its pale stucco walls and Native American wall hangings faded into nonexistence.

Ben's cologne was subtle and very masculine. His bolo tie was straight...his shoulders so very wide. The Western-cut jacket fit him perfectly. She wondered about the man inside. What did he really think about her pregnancy? How did he actually feel? When she'd spoken to him the night of the engagement party, she'd known he was a guarded man. That guard covered his emotions.

Sierra could feel Ben's fingers through the chiffon. Her dress was two pieces, a long flowing jacket with long sleeves, ruffles on the cuffs, and a slip of a dress underneath. Now it seemed almost like a second skin as the dance floor grew more crowded and Ben pulled her a little closer. She looked up and became immobilized by his stormy gray eyes.

She almost tripped when they moved, and he caught her even tighter. "Are you okay?"

"Fine." This near, she couldn't help thinking about their bodies joining seven weeks ago.

He must have been thinking about it, too, because he said, "I want you to understand something, Sierra. What happened at the engagement party wasn't an everyday happening for me, either. I have never slept with a woman without protection before." His voice was low, his face close to hers.

"Even when you're in a relationship?"

His brow furrowed, and she knew he wasn't going to confide in her about any of those relationships. "Even in a relationship. A relationship isn't a marriage. A child deserves two parents who are committed to each other."

In a way, his statement was reassuring. But in another way, that intensity she sensed in Ben would be directed toward his child, toward fathering, toward custody.

He went on, "I don't usually sleep that soundly, either. I hadn't gotten much sleep that week or I would have heard you when you left. I wouldn't have let you leave."

"What would you have done?"

For a moment he was silent and she guessed he was trying to find diplomatic words. "I would have gotten your number in case anything happened. I take my responsibilities seriously. This baby, if it's mine, will be my responsibility."

"*I'm* the one who's carrying this child. I'll be primary caregiver. I'll be making decisions for me and the baby."

When he stiffened, she knew she might have been too blunt. But they might as well set their boundaries now. She wasn't going to take directives or follow orders. If he wanted to be involved, this was about both of them being parents, not one or the other taking control.

After a few more seconds of their bodies not being as relaxed as they were a few moments before, Ben said, "I should break in on Camille and Miguel. That's the tradition. Let's move that way."

She couldn't tell if he'd had enough close contact or was really concerned about tradition. But she let him lead her toward the newly married couple.

Ben tapped his friend on the shoulder. "I think it's my turn. You'll have her for the rest of your life."

"And I'll even miss these few minutes with her," Miguel complained. But then he looked at Sierra. Smiling, he offered her his hand. "Dancing with you will be my pleasure."

He floated her away comfortably, not at all awkwardly the way she and Ben had danced. On second thought, the tension had been awkward, but their bodies had fit together all too well.

"So," Miguel said, studying her carefully. "Camille tells me you and Ben arrived together. Are we supposed to read something into that?"

"There's nothing to read. Why should both of us drive up separately?"

"That's what I told Camille. But you know her, she has

a suspicious nature. She maintains you two disappeared the night of our engagement party and we're seeing the results of that now."

"The results of what?" she asked.

"That's what Camille wants to know."

"You have no interest, of course." Sierra gave him a rueful smile.

"Let's just say, not many women turn Ben Barclay's head."

"How long have you been friends?" Sierra asked, eager to know more.

"Camille never told you our history?"

Sierra had avoided asking Camille questions about Ben. She hadn't wanted to seem too interested. Actually, she hadn't been interested. Not until they'd started talking, not until—

"No, she never told me."

"Ben went to college with my brother." A look of pain settled on Miguel's face, pain that was always in his heart.

Sierra had known that Miguel's brother, Pablo, had been killed in a drive-by shooting when he was home from college one summer.

"Ben was with Pablo when he was shot."

Miguel never talked about his brother and Sierra had never asked. Camille had told her the basics and she hadn't pressed for more.

Continuing, he explained, "Ben had come home with Pablo for a vacation before they both went to Tennessee to work on Habitat for Humanity homes. I really think what happened to my brother was the reason Ben decided to be a prosecutor, why he came here to Albuquerque instead of going back to his home in Minnesota."

Miguel gave her a sad smile. "He has two brothers back home, but he's become the brother to me that I lost. That's why he's my best man, and..." Miguel paused for effect. "That's how I know there's a spark in his eye when he looks at you. I haven't seen that for a very long time."

If Sierra asked Miguel more questions about Ben, he might answer her. For instance, when had he last seen that spark? Yet she knew if she wanted the answer, she would have to ask Ben herself. She needed to see his expression, learn to know him on her own.

"Ben doesn't give much away, does he?" she asked.

"Think about his job, Sierra. Think about what he does every day, the criminals he has to question. Think about the juries he has to convince, the trials he has to win to make everyone safe. He's practiced hard at giving nothing away. You'll be good for him. You wear your heart on your sleeve. That's a compliment, by the way, so don't be offended. That was one thing I liked about you as soon as Camille introduced us—your lack of pretense."

As the song ended, Miguel guided Sierra to where Camille and Ben were standing. Miguel took his new wife into his arms again. "How about one more dance before we start mingling?"

Camille gave him a kiss in reply.

Ben said to Sierra, "I'm going to step out on the balcony for some fresh air."

She didn't know if it was an invitation or not, but she took it as one. "That sounds like a good idea."

They walked side by side to the French doors that led to a long balcony. He opened the door for her, and when they stepped outside, she realized they were alone. Although

Sierra took in a deep lungful of the crisper night air, pleasant after the stuffiness inside, the breeze made her shiver.

"Cold?" Ben asked as a loose strand of her hair brushed against her cheek with the breeze.

"A little, but it feels good." They were standing at the wrought-iron railing looking up at a magnificent night sky.

Ben reached over and touched her hand. "You *are* cold." He shrugged out of his jacket and settled it around her shoulders.

She could feel his body heat still warming it and sank into the scent of his cologne. She asked, "Have you ever ridden a cable car up to the top of Sandia Peak at night?" She often took advantage of the tourist attraction when she needed to go to the top of the world and think.

"I've been up there a couple of times, but not at night."

"You have to go. With the lights of Albuquerque below, the stars and the moon up above, it's like being suspended in space where anything's possible."

They were silent again for a few minutes and then Ben turned to look at her. The light from inside the inn played over him, casting half his face in shadow. "You said you hadn't been with a man for a long time. How long?"

"Since I was twenty."

If he was surprised, he didn't let on. Instead he asked a perceptive question. "What happened when you were twenty?"

She didn't want to go there, she really didn't, but she'd already sensed Ben wouldn't give his trust easily. She wanted him to trust her. How else could they be parents together? "It's still difficult for me to remember."

When he kept quiet, she had no idea what he was

thinking. Concerned he'd mistakenly believe she'd been assaulted or worse, she quickly said, "After high school I wasn't sure what I wanted to do. So I returned to Africa where my parents were then to help reestablish our relationship. I hadn't seen them much over those four years. I thought if I acted as their secretary or assistant, maybe we could finally connect now that I was an adult."

"Did that happen?"

"No. They really didn't need me. I volunteered at a medical center. I was drawn to the children there and got to know the doctor who set up the clinic."

"Got to know him?"

"Fell in love with him. Six months later we were planning our wedding. A week before the ceremony, he learned of an epidemic in one of the villages. He was determined to go and save lives and wouldn't let me go with him. The reason was, there were guerrillas in the area, guerrillas who don't care about sick children or the doctors who help them. All they cared about was stealing supplies and taking what they needed. Travis went because saving lives came first before any personal considerations. I knew if he was needed there, we'd postpone the wedding. I understood that. I understood his need to help."

"What happened?"

"Travis was killed by fanatics who didn't care who they murdered." Her voice shook and she could hear the quiver. Tears burned in her eyes, and because she didn't want Ben to see them, she stared up at the sky again.

"It seems like yesterday?" he asked in a low voice.

"Sometimes. Other times, it feels like a lifetime ago." She slipped his coat from her shoulders, suddenly needing to be away from him, away from a man who stirred up feelings she hadn't experienced in a very long time, away from a man who had wiped Travis from her memories for an evening.

She blinked a few times and found a smile and handed him his jacket. "Thanks. I think I'll go in now."

He didn't stop her as she opened the door and stepped back into the reception.

Sierra mingled for a while, wanting to forget about her discussion with Ben on the balcony, not wanting to stir up memories of Travis or even the electrically charged feeling she experienced whenever she was with Ben. After speaking for a while with Miguel's parents and then Camille's, she noticed Ben on the other side of the room talking to a man who looked to be about his age. At the dessert table the wedding cake just didn't tempt her, so she picked up one of the other selections, a cup of crème brûlée, and carried it to her table. She took a few bites.

Camille slipped onto the seat beside her. "Did you and Ben have a good conversation out on the balcony? It's a romantic night out there."

Sierra could see her friend was teasing her. She should tell her about her pregnancy. "We talked."

"What aren't you telling me?"

"Camille, this is your wedding night. Why would you care what we talked about? You should be thinking about later, leaving tomorrow morning on your honeymoon."

"Oh, I am, but you know me, I can multitask."

Knowing her friend deserved the honesty with which they usually spoke, Sierra said, "I told him about Travis."

Camille studied her. "There's more going on here than two people who just met each other."

That was an opening, so Sierra took it. Leaning close to Camille, she murmured in her ear, "I'm pregnant. Ben's the father. I wasn't going to tell you now, but you're pushing."

Camille tried to recover from her astonishment. "You *are* going to tell me when, where, how and why."

"Not now, not here. I just told Ben last week. I want you to forget about it until you get back from your honeymoon."

Camille laid her hand on her friend's shoulder. "Are you all right?"

Although the crème brûlée was lying heavy in her stomach, she assured Camille, "I'm fine. I'm going to figure it all out."

"With Ben's help?"

"We'll see."

Camille whistled through her teeth. "Ben Barclay. Who would have thought?"

Sierra's quelling look didn't intimidate Camille. "So *that's* why you told him about Travis. Was that so you could get closer to him or push him away?"

Her friend never ducked the hard questions and Sierra had to think about that one. "I'm not sure."

Her stomach felt even queasier. To distract both of them, she swiveled in her chair to face Camille. "So describe this resort where you're staying in Aruba."

"You're changing the subject."

"You bet I am."

"It's supposed to have everything, but Miguel and I probably won't be seeing the outside of our room. I can't wait to have nine whole days with him, without interruptions, without hi-and-goodbye schedules. I'm glad I quit my job last month to help with the wedding details. I know it will help us get a good start on our marriage."

As an art history major, Camille had been working in

one of the galleries in Santa Fe since she graduated from college. "Do you think you'll go back to work?"

"Miguel doesn't want me to. We'd really like to start a family, but I think part-time work might be nice. We'll see how things go until after the New Year."

Miguel was vice president at one of the Santa Fe banks. He'd also inherited a trust fund from his grandmother, so if Camille didn't want to go back to work, they didn't have to worry. But if Camille didn't get pregnant quickly, Sierra suspected she'd tire of being a stay-at-home wife.

The nausea Sierra experienced was increasing, becoming more intense.

Camille studied her. "You're looking a little green."

Suddenly Sierra knew she needed to make an exit to the bathroom and fast. "Be right back," she managed to mumble as she hopped up from her chair and made a beeline toward the ladies' room. She just made it in time into one of the stalls and lost her supper when Camille rushed in after her.

"Are you okay? Ben's right outside, he's worried."

Sierra stood and took a deep breath. Actually she felt much better. Pushing the door open, she told Camille, "I'm fine now, really," and went to the sink to wash her face.

There was a knock on the ladies' room door.

Camille's brows arched just as the door opened an inch and one very masculine voice demanded, "Sierra? Are you all right? Can I come in?"

Seeing Ben right now was the *last* thing Sierra wanted.

Chapter Four

It had been a very long time since Ben had worried about anyone besides his brothers and his father, took care of anyone or even wanted to. But he found himself wanting to take care of Sierra.

Because she might be carrying his baby?

That was it, of course.

"Don't let him in!"

Ben heard Sierra's plea to Camille as he stood outside the ladies' room door. Her words ratcheted up his concern.

Opening the door a little wider, he asked calmly, although he wasn't feeling calm, "What's wrong, Sierra?"

Camille stepped in front of him. "She's cleaning up. Give her a minute."

Ben peered around Camille and saw Sierra at the sink, water dripping from her face, a drop or two falling on her beautiful gown.

She groaned. "I don't want anyone to see me like this." After she glanced at Ben in the mirror, she must have realized her wish to be alone wouldn't keep him out. She sighed and explained, "I shouldn't have eaten the crème brûlée." She produced a weak smile, took a paper towel and dabbed at the droplets on her face. Then she looked down at her gown. "I've made a mess."

She looked like a little kid who'd dropped ice cream on her shoe, and he was ready to take a few steps toward her when Sierra's face suddenly turned a little greener and she made a beeline for the bathroom cubicle again.

Camille whispered to him, "Don't embarrass her. Let me handle this."

He didn't want to let Camille handle this. No one else handled his responsibilities but him. But then he thought about Sierra, her pale face, her weak smile, the way she'd left his room because everything had become too intense.

He always knew what to do, and he hated the fact he was teetering on the brink of indecision now. "Five minutes," he agreed. "I'll wait outside for five minutes. But if you're not out, I'm coming in. I'm taking her to a doctor if I have to."

"She doesn't need a doctor," Camille assured him with a shake of her head. "She just needs some soda and a few crackers. Men. If they had to have babies—"

"Okay, I won't stay for the lecture." With a last look at the bathroom stall, he closed the door to the ladies' room to wait.

The five minutes were almost up when both Sierra and Camille stepped outside the door. Sierra was holding her purse, twisting the silver chain. "I'm fine."

She did *not* look fine. He remembered her high color

that day in his office, as well as upstairs in the bedroom. She was unnaturally pale and looked a little shaky.

"I'm taking you back to the hacienda."

Sierra turned to Camille. "I don't want to leave the reception."

"I'm just going to throw the bouquet and then we're off, too," she said. Gently taking Sierra by the elbow, she guided her to a chair at the periphery of the room. "Do you need to sit for a few minutes?"

When Sierra shook her head, Ben had the illogical, irrational desire to sweep her up into his arms and carry her to the car. How crazy was that?

"I'll tell Mrs. Padilla and my mom that you went back to the hacienda," Camille said. "Elena's there. She left a little while ago. She'll let you in."

Elena was the Padillas' housekeeper who also kept the home fires burning. She was Val's age and in lots of ways reminded Ben of Nathan's housekeeper. They both cared deeply about the families they took care of.

Five minutes later as Ben and Sierra left the inn, Ben took off his jacket and draped it around her shoulders again to keep her warm in the cool night air. After he went to retrieve his SUV and pulled up in front, the doorman helped Sierra inside.

She settled in, fastened her seat belt and laid her head back against the headrest. "I'm sorry this happened. I should have known better."

"Does this happen often?"

"No, just when I eat something too rich—cheesecake, crème brûlée. I guess I'll be eating healthy throughout my pregnancy."

"Are you sure it's normal?"

"*Normal* is a relative term with pregnancy. Some women crave peanut butter and pickles and feel fine when they eat them. Some women crave tuna fish and can't keep it down. Some women feel sick the first three months and some not at all. There's no right or wrong, rhyme nor reason."

"My brother's wife has been craving banana and mayonnaise sandwiches her whole pregnancy."

Sierra groaned. "Oh, please."

He laughed. "Sorry."

The drive to the hacienda only took about ten minutes. After Elena let them in, Sierra headed upstairs while Ben went to the kitchen with the housekeeper, remembering what Camille had said. He filled a glass with ice, added soda and asked Elena for crackers. Then he took the whole package along with the soda up to Sierra's room and knocked.

"Just a minute," she called.

When she opened the door, she was barefoot with a cream silk robe wrapped around her. He couldn't tell for sure, but he thought he could make out the outline of her bra and panties underneath.

"I'm…I'm not dressed for visitors," she said lightly. Her face had regained some of its color.

"I'm not a visitor. I think we're past that. I brought you soda and crackers. Camille thought that might help."

Breaking eye contact, he took the snack over to the nightstand and set it down. "Why don't you slip under the covers?" he suggested. "You might feel more comfortable that way."

"You're staying?" Her voice was surprised and a little thin.

"I just want to make sure you're really okay."

"And how long do you think it will take for you to find out?" she asked cheekily.

"I guess I'll be able to tell if you drink some soda and eat some crackers and don't go all pale and sick again."

She still didn't get into bed. "I've never had a keeper, Ben. I don't really want one now."

He realized she'd been on her own most of her childhood and supposed she'd gotten used to going where she wanted to go and doing what she wanted to do. "If you don't want a keeper, why do you still live with your aunt?"

"You're *really* not going to leave?" she asked with a sigh.

"Really not."

He stepped away from the nightstand so she could pull back the covers and crawl in. She left on her robe, but he got a glimpse of thigh and leg that made his groin tighten.

"Don't loom," she warned him.

Hiding a smile, he lowered himself to the bed next to her hip, then realized exactly how intimate their positions were. They were in her bedroom. She was barely dressed, and he was very close. Close enough that he could smell a minty scent. He suspected the first thing she'd done when she reached her room was brush her teeth.

Now she took one of the crackers and nibbled on it. He kept silent until she'd finished because she still hadn't answered his question.

"Your aunt?" he asked again.

"I live with my aunt because I feel connected to her. I'm her only family except for my parents and she's mine. She invested in my shop to get me started and I'll always be grateful for that. I paid her back last year," Sierra added proudly. "I talked about moving out, even looked at apartments, but she always has a reason for me to stay. The last time I was ready to put down a security deposit she said she was taking this trip. If I were at her house, she wouldn't have to worry about someone checking on it every day. It made sense." Sierra took a few sips of soda, then set down her glass.

"Family does have a grounding quality. I can understand why you're so close to your aunt…how she's looked out for you through the years. My brothers and I do that for each other. Nathan called before the wedding. He was checking with me to see if I wanted him and Sara and Kyle to fly in for Thanksgiving."

Sierra's beautiful blue eyes widened. "Do you?"

"Yes, I do. I have too much work to fly to Minnesota for the holiday, so this plan is a good one. Maybe you can meet them."

She looked worried. "Do they know?"

"I told Nathan. He'll tell the others. I'm sure I'll be hearing from my brother Sam and my father."

She looked thoughtfully at him. "Was your dad a good role model?"

"The best. Maybe not right after my mother left. He was bitter, distracted, and he seemed to be living in another universe some days. But I had Sam and Nathan and eventually he snapped out of it. He built a cabin up north and we went there to fish and cross-country ski and hike. We became a different family up there."

"Different?"

"Yeah, no mom. But we figured out we didn't need one. We were good together. After we started spending time there, Dad was with us. Know what I mean? Always there. We knew we could count on him and one another."

"It was terrible losing your mom, but the rest sounds really great. I worry that—"

It was obvious that Sierra was in turmoil about something and he wanted to know what it was. He inched a little closer to her hip and leaned nearer to her. "What do you worry about?"

After biting her lower lip, she blurted out, "I'm afraid I won't have motherly instincts. I'm afraid I'll be like my own mother. That sounds terrible. It's just—You said your dad was there. My mom wasn't. My mom and dad were this unit that I couldn't break into. So I guess bonding with a child doesn't always come naturally and I'm afraid. What if I don't bond?"

Ben wasn't the least bit worried about Sierra's mothering skills. "I saw you with Camille's niece this afternoon, remember? You reacted like a mother would. You didn't make her feel bad about running into you, but you told her what she needed to hear."

"You were watching that closely?"

"I have a vested interest."

Sierra's eyes were so shiny and big and full of vulnerability, and her face had regained its color. He only leaned forward to give her a little reassurance. He only leaned forward to place a light kiss on her lips. But that light kiss became need.

Her lips clung to his and her hands came up to grasp his shoulders. Realizing the need wasn't just one-sided—she seemed to need him, too—he let his desire command the kiss. They'd kissed before, but this was a conscious kiss, a kiss filled with everything that could still happen between them.

Did he *want* anything to happen? He hadn't fully

absorbed the idea of fatherhood yet. He still hadn't decided whether or not Sierra was playing him, whether she was what she seemed, whether she might include him freely in her life and their child's or cut him out. He didn't know any of it and he'd better be damn careful until he did.

Cutting off the kiss, he stood. He was getting out of this room and away from her so he could think clearly.

But before either of them could utter a word, Ben's phone beeped. He'd turned it off during the wedding, but switched it back on during the reception.

When his gaze met Sierra's, her color was high, her lips swollen with a just-kissed look that tempted him to kiss her all over again. Instead, he checked his caller ID. "I have to get this," he said tersely.

She just nodded, maybe even looked a bit relieved.

"Barclay," he said when he answered.

"Ben, it's Vince."

Vince Rossi was a detective with the Albuquerque police force. He and Ben had worked closely on a few cases.

"What's up?"

"You had a prowler."

"What do you mean, I had a prowler?"

"At your house. Your neighbor called it in. She got a good look. Apparently the guy ducked under the streetlight before he ran behind the fence. He was about five eight, dark hair, long nose, pointed chin, sideburns. Any ideas?"

"Long hair and sideburns? I can't be sure, but it sounds like Charlie Levsin's brother, Al. He—" Ben hesitated because he knew Sierra was listening. "He and I had a conversation in a mall parking lot Friday night."

"He jumped you?"

"Nothing physical."

"He warned you off the case?"

"Something like that."

"And you didn't tell anyone?"

"What was there to say?"

Vince blew out a breath. "Do you want me to check the house?"

"In the back of the house, there's a key on a magnet on the underside of the grill."

"You're a D.A. Do you think that's inventive?"

"I thought it was obvious enough so no one would look."

"Right," Vince drawled sarcastically. "I'll check around, get back to you if I see anything that shouldn't be there, or looks like it's been moved. When are you coming home?"

"Tomorrow."

"Give me a call after you get in. Let me know if you see anything I didn't."

"Thanks, Vince."

"No problem."

When Ben clicked off and closed his phone, Sierra was studying him. "You had a break-in?"

He wasn't going to lie to her, but he didn't want to make it more than it was, either. "No, the neighbor just thought she saw a prowler."

"*Thought* she saw? It sounded like she had a description."

"What did you do, take notes while I was talking?"

She waved away his sarcasm. "If you know who it might be, then something's going on. What?"

"It's just business as usual, Sierra. I'm involved in a case. Some people would like me to lose it."

"Some people would break into your home while you're not there? Or some people wished you might have been there?" She looked shocked and upset at what she'd deduced.

He'd intended to get out of her room fast, but now he couldn't. He could see that. He took a step toward her, but only a step. "This is my job, Sierra. I put bad guys away. They don't go by the same rules normal people do."

"Don't patronize me, Ben. I guess I never realized an A.D.A.'s job could be dangerous, as well as life consuming." She closed her eyes and murmured, "I never wanted to get involved with someone in a dangerous job, in a job that meant more than…than everything else."

"Being parents together doesn't mean we have to be involved."

Her eyes blinked open and she stared at him with what looked like hurt.

Damn, he hadn't meant to do that, but they *weren't* involved. And maybe they shouldn't be.

With a sigh, he rubbed the back of his neck and crossed to the door. He gestured to the nightstand. "Don't forget about the soda and crackers." She might be the mother of his child so he *had* to care about her well-being, didn't he? "And if you don't feel well during the night, or you need anything, call me. Do you still have my number?"

"I do. But I won't need anything, Ben. I can take care of myself and my baby without your help."

There really wasn't anything else to say. They'd both come away from the kiss rattled, and the phone call hadn't helped.

After he opened the door, he said, "I'll see you in the morning."

She nodded. "In the morning."

As Ben left Sierra's room, he felt as if something had gone terribly wrong. It hadn't been the kiss or even what he'd said about not being involved. It had been the phone call.

His work was going to be an obstacle just as it had been to other relationships. But he had to do his job. His work was the most important thing in his life right now.

Except for being a dad, the voice of his conscience reminded him.

Except for being a dad.

The return drive from Santa Fe to Albuquerque the following morning was silent. Sierra glanced over at Ben as he parked in front of her aunt's house and opened his car door.

"You don't have to come in."

"You were gone overnight. I'll just make sure everything's the way it should be, then I'll leave."

He'd seemed removed through breakfast this morning. But she hadn't said anything and told herself not to press him…told herself she was *not* falling for Ben Barclay.

Once they walked through the wrought-iron gate in the house's protective adobe wall, Sierra unlocked the door, slipped inside and deactivated the alarm. She forced a smile. "See, everything's good."

"Sierra, about last night—"

She kept up the airy facade. "Thanks for bringing me the soda and crackers. I guess Miguel and Camille are on a plane right now on their way to Aruba. I hope the weather's good—"

Ben came even closer. "I know the phone call rattled you."

Obviously he wasn't going to leave until he discussed what he wanted to discuss. "Didn't it rattle you?" she returned.

"No. All of it's just part of my job," he said again.

"How can you be so matter-of-fact about someone prowling around your house?"

"Because I have to put it out of my head, think about the strategies for the trial and nothing else."

"Is that what you were doing this morning?"

"This morning?"

"Yes. You hardly said two words at breakfast. Miguel's mother was trying to have a conversation with you and it just didn't happen. In the car you were silent for the whole drive. Either you didn't want me there beside you, or you had something major on your mind. Since we're *not* personally involved, it can't have anything to do with *us,* but I thought it might have something to do with the baby."

Ben ran his hand through his hair. "Sierra—" He blew out a breath. "I'm not used to having to explain myself to anyone. My life isn't amenable to relationships. I've always been a loner."

"You said you were close to your brothers."

"I am, but I've always needed my own time, my own space. My family may ask questions, but when I don't answer them, they accept that. But I have a feeling that you won't. I can't tell you everything I was thinking."

"Because it has to do with the trial?" she guessed.

"Yes."

"And the rest?" Obviously Ben wasn't used to sharing his thoughts, and she hoped that would change.

"Let's face it. You've had a little more time to absorb the parent thing than I have. We've got a lot of decisions to make."

"Such as?"

"Whether or not we'll share joint custody."

She was startled and suddenly stricken. Maybe she'd been naive, but she'd never believed her having full custody would be an issue, especially taking Ben's job into consideration. She really *didn't* know Ben. He *was* a lawyer. Would he want more than joint custody? He couldn't take her baby from her, could he? What if he had connections that could assure whatever decree he wanted?

Was *this* what he'd been considering on the drive home? "You aren't serious!"

"I'm *very* serious."

She couldn't imagine loving a child, caring for a child, yet giving that baby up part of the week, month or year. She supposed she'd told Ben about the pregnancy simply to have him as a male presence in the baby's life if he wanted to be. "There's no way we can have joint custody when you work the way you do."

"I'm not talking about half the time at my place and half at yours. I'm talking about joint custody on all decisions, me having a say in my child's life, me spending time, as much time as I can with a son or daughter."

She turned away from him, wondering if she'd made the biggest mistake of her life telling him about the pregnancy. She'd only wanted to do the right thing.

He nudged her around. "I want to be included in my baby's life, and we have to figure out the best way for that to happen. If we make unilateral decisions, both of us will regret it."

Would they? She wasn't so sure.

Suddenly he looked wary and concerned, his eyes troubled. "You weren't thinking of running, were you?"

The truth was, when she thought about some judge deciding their baby's fate she *had* thought about leaving Albuquerque. But she was more responsible than that. She had a business and employees. "I have a life here, Ben. I make a good living. I'd be a fool to leave that. Besides, I want what's best for the baby. Two parents would be better than one. It's just— When I found out I was pregnant, I envisioned *me* being a mother. By myself."

When he placed a hand on each of her shoulders, she felt the heat of them as she looked directly into his eyes. "You're not alone, Sierra, not anymore. We're going to do this together."

Did he have any idea of how complicated that could be? Unless he had no feelings at all for her. Maybe that was it. This would be easy for him if he could stay removed. The problem was—she didn't think *she* could stay removed from *him,* even though that would be best, even though his job was a barrier, even though his work could be dangerous in spite of his protestations otherwise. She liked Ben, admired him, melted whenever she thought about him touching her.

He had said they weren't involved. Yet the way he was looking at her… His eyes had darkened the night of the engagement party as they'd talked, just before he'd kissed her. They were darkening now in that same way.

But then he released her and dropped his hands to his sides. His eyes were still darker, but his expression went stone-faced. He was hiding everything he was thinking and feeling. How could he do that so effectively?

"I have to go," he said gruffly.

"I do, too. I want to make the noon service at church." It was already eleven-thirty.

"What church?"

"Our Lady of Guadalupe."

He didn't seem to know what to say to that. "You're going to drive?"

"Sure am. I have my own car. It's parked around back. Do you go to church?" she asked.

"Now and then."

"But not often because you have work to do on weekends," she guessed.

"Usually."

Neither of them seemed to know what to add, neither of them knew when they'd see each other again, until Sierra suddenly remembered. "My doctor's appointment is on Thursday at eleven o'clock at Dr. Connor's office. She's on San Mateo."

"Do you still want me to be there?"

"Only if you want to be."

"I might not know until the last minute if I can get away."

"That's fine. If you're there, you're there. If you aren't, you aren't." She tried to make it sound as if his commitment to the appointment didn't matter at all.

He frowned. "All right. Maybe I'll see you on Thursday."

After he went to the door and opened it, he took a last look at her and then left.

Sierra felt as if she'd handled everything all wrong, but

she didn't know how she could have handled it differently. She couldn't make Ben care about her. She didn't even know if she *wanted* him to care about her. She realized again that she was more attracted to him than she'd ever been to a man, even Travis.

And that upset her most of all.

Chapter Five

Ben hadn't come.

"Go ahead and get dressed," Dr. Connor said after examining Sierra. "When you're finished, come over to my office."

After the door closed, Sierra stepped down from the table and began dressing. The disappointment that Ben hadn't met her here was deeper than it should be. He was a busy man. It was the middle of the day. This appointment wasn't anything crucial.

Did Ben believe yet that she was carrying *his* child? He seemed to at times, but then at others… That hard look came into his eyes, a look that said he'd trusted before and had been hurt, a look that said he wouldn't be taking any chances again.

She hadn't heard from him since he'd brought her home from the wedding on Sunday.

But then why should she?

A rap on the door broke her train of thought. Sierra had pulled on her red broomstick skirt and buttoned her patterned blouse when the nurse peeked in. "Mr. Barclay is here, but I just showed him to the doctor's office and said you'd be there in a minute. Is that okay?"

"Fine," she managed to say, fastening the concho belt around her waist. Slipping into her shoes, quickly running a brush through her hair, she hurried to the doctor's office.

Ben was pacing, his long strides telling her the room wasn't wide enough for where he wanted to go.

She stepped inside, but before she could even greet him, he said, "I got tied up with a deposition. Did everything go okay?" He sounded worried and his concern made her relax a bit.

"Everything's fine."

The doctor suddenly came in and smiled at the two of them. She was a woman in her late fifties with black hair streaked with gray and green eyes that sparkled with intelligence and caring.

Sierra made the introductions. "Dr. Connor, this is Ben Barclay. He's the father."

Dr. Connor didn't miss a beat, just shook Ben's hand and greeted him warmly. Then she went to sit behind her desk. "I know Sierra wanted you here today in case you had any questions."

A gentleman clear through, Ben waited until Sierra took a seat in one of the two chairs in front of the desk before he sat in the other. With their arms almost brushing, she felt the intense magnetism that had drawn her to him in the first place. But he didn't seem to be affected by her or the doctor's office or anything else. That was Ben, all stoic control.

A teasing little voice whispered, *Not when he makes love.*

Ben drowned out the little voice when he said, "Sierra tells me she'll be seeing you once a month."

"That's right. Until the last trimester, then we'll switch to bimonthly and then weekly appointments."

"Will you do an ultrasound?"

"Yes, at about twenty weeks. I know you're probably looking forward to seeing a picture of your child, but I feel that's the best time to do it unless there's a problem."

"I did have a question about paternity testing. Is amniocentesis the only way to do that in utero?"

Ben's question surprised Sierra and also embarrassed her. The implied message was that he wanted to know if he was the father. The implied message was that he didn't believe Sierra when she said he was. She felt her cheeks warming and her mouth going dry.

"There is another test that utilizes the placenta—chorionic villus sampling," the doctor replied, looking from Ben to Sierra and back to him again. "At Sierra's age, amnio isn't necessary. With it, there's always the risk of miscarriage. And as for the CVS, any tampering with a pregnancy is never one-hundred-percent safe. But if you want either…"

"I don't want to do anything to disrupt the pregnancy," Ben assured the physician. "We can wait until after the baby's born."

"Then a paternity test will be no problem at all," the doctor concluded.

While Ben asked a few more questions concerning Sierra's due date, the possibility that the baby would be early or late, Sierra didn't pay that much attention. Her embarrassment shifted into anger and she just wanted to leave the doctor's office and get some air.

A few minutes later they were standing outside the medical center, the sun beating hard on their shoulders.

Sierra turned to Ben before he could walk away to his car. "Why did you embarrass me like that in front of Dr. Connor? She's an old friend of my aunt's."

"Embarrass you? You told me to come if I had questions. I had questions."

"I could have inquired about the DNA test much more subtly. You didn't have to humiliate me in front of her."

"How did I humiliate you? I just asked a question."

"No. What you implied is that you don't trust my word about this child being yours."

His brows furrowed and he appeared to be perplexed. "Look, Sierra, in what I do every day, only the bottom line matters. I'm not used to beating around the bush. When I have a question, I ask it. After the baby's born, we'll take care of the DNA test."

Sierra just stared at him. She'd opened up to him. She'd told him about Travis and her childhood, but apparently none of that mattered. He still thought she slept around, had dates every weekend and didn't know who she did what with or when. And there was only one reason for that.

"I know your mother left and that created a big issue with your ability to trust. But I don't think that's the only reason. What is?"

When Ben remained silent, she could see how firmly set in place his guard was. He wasn't going to let it down, not even for her. That was definitely the best reason why falling for him would be a monumental mistake.

Whether hormones were driving her or her own emotions, she didn't know, but she felt close to tears and she wasn't going to let him see her cry. "I guess we really don't need to see each other again until after the baby's born," she suddenly decided. "I'll call you when I go into labor."

Spinning around, she quickly walked toward her car. He didn't come after her.

Ben felt nervous, a nervousness he'd never experienced before as he stood at Sierra's door and rang her bell. He wished he felt as confident as he did in a courtroom. He wasn't exactly sure what had happened this afternoon at the doctor's office, but something had. Had he really humiliated Sierra?

When she'd left him in the parking lot, he'd felt as if she'd slipped through his fingers, like he'd lost her, and that was really crazy because they weren't even together. They didn't even know each other. That was the crux of the matter.

He jabbed her doorbell, knowing it was late for a visit—9:00 p.m. He'd been going over detective reports and that had taken a lot longer than he'd planned.

When Sierra opened the door, he imagined she'd already peered through the peephole. Her expression was completely bland as if she'd arranged her face to give no hint of what she was feeling. He'd never seen that look on her before. She was wearing a robe, not the silky traveling robe she'd taken to the hacienda, but a substantial bright pink chenille one. Her hand was on her belt making sure it was tied tightly.

"Can I come in?" he asked when she just stood there.

"That depends," she answered, looking him straight in the eye. "Am I going to be glad you're here, or sorry you came?"

He almost smiled…almost. "I don't know. I guess it depends on how the conversation goes. We won't know unless you let me in."

Her expression still didn't change, though he thought he saw a hint of amusement in her eyes. She backed up and opened the door wider. He stepped inside and closed the door behind him. He could see she'd been lounging on the sofa. A magazine was open and some kind of box with beads in it was perched on top of it.

"Are you working?"

"Just playing with some designs."

As he stepped closer to the sofa he spotted a felt board with two semicircular channels lined with several shapes of beads. Soft strains of guitar music played in the room.

"So why did you come by?" Sierra prompted without asking him to sit.

"I want to apologize if I embarrassed you this afternoon at the doctor's. I never meant to do that."

After she studied him for a moment, she motioned him to the sofa. "I was just going to get myself some apple juice and cookies. Are you interested?"

Actually, he'd skipped supper and he was interested in anything edible. "That would be great. Need help?"

Before she could say no, he followed her into the kitchen. Brows arched, a smile quirking up the corners of her lips, she pointed to the decorative can on the counter. "Sugar cookies are in there. Just bring the can."

"They agree with you?"

"Absolutely. I can eat them anytime, day or night." She took a half-gallon jug of apple juice from the refrigerator, collected two glasses and poured.

"Mind if I snatch a banana?" he asked, eyeing the fruit bowl on the counter.

Now she did smile. "I don't mind. Did you skip supper? I can make you a sandwich."

"I don't want you to go to any trouble."

"No trouble. It will just take a minute."

Ten minutes later, he'd finished the sandwich and the banana while she'd gathered her beading supplies and mounded them on the coffee table.

After a few swigs of apple juice, he suggested, "I owe you dinner sometime."

"Quid pro quo for a sandwich?"

"No. I just want to take you to dinner." An awkward silence settled between them and he knew he had to break it. "My track record with women isn't good."

"Your fault or theirs?"

He shook his head and chuckled. "You don't let anything pass, do you?"

"I don't think we're that different, Ben. You want to know the bottom line and so do I."

"Score one for you," he muttered, wondering why she unsettled him more than any other woman ever had, as well as turned him on. He didn't see a nightgown peeking out from under that robe and his imagination was going wild from envisioning what was or wasn't under it.

"Ben?" she asked.

He took a sugar cookie from the can, toyed with the edge, took a couple of bites, then set the rest of it on the napkin on the table in front of him.

Sierra was sitting beside him on the sofa, and they were practically knee to knee. He'd gotten rid of his tie and suitcoat in the car and unbuttoned the top buttons of his shirt. But he still felt constricted in some way, uncomfortable, unwilling to shake out an unsuccessful romantic past and show it to Sierra.

"My work has always gotten in the way."

"Always?"

He knew what she meant. What had happened before the work had come along?

"In high school I played sports to try to earn scholarships—basketball and track. When I wasn't at practice, I had a job at a grocery store packing bags. My brothers and I wanted to go to college, and we knew we couldn't burden Dad with tuition costs. I believed I couldn't get serious about anybody for a long time because I had to focus on school, sports and my job."

"So you went out with girls who weren't serious?"

"Yeah, I went out with girls who didn't want strings any more than I did. The same with college. I had a job and needed to get good grades to get into law school." He stopped.

As if she was reading his mind, as if she knew what would come next, she admitted, "Miguel told me about you and Pablo."

"Recently?"

"When we danced at the wedding reception."

Ben frowned. "You were discussing me?"

Although Sierra looked a bit embarrassed, she shrugged. "Miguel wanted to know what was going on—why we'd come to the wedding together. I asked how long he'd known you and he told me."

After a pause, Ben admitted, "That summer changed my life. Before that, I'd thought about going into corporate law, maybe international law. But after that drive-by shooting—I knew I had to do something that mattered more."

She leaned forward a little closer now as if she were

intensely interested in what he was saying. "What you do couldn't be any more important."

When their eyes held, he felt something so deep inside he couldn't name it. It wasn't just desire. It wasn't just liking. It was some kind of connection that he'd never experienced with a woman before. And the truth was, it shook him even more than facing a criminal who was destined for life imprisonment.

Clasping his hands, he let them drop between his thighs, staring at them. He knew why he'd never done this kind of thing before. He hated tearing off a piece of his soul and bringing it out into the light. That's what it felt like he was doing.

"But you did have a serious relationship?" she guessed.

Did he really *want* to do this? The more information Sierra had about him, the more power she held in her hands. He knew that. It went along with not asking a question he couldn't answer. When someone was on the witness stand, information was always power.

"Why is this so hard for you?" she asked softly.

"Because I'm a private person."

"Yes, you are, but I think this is more about talking through something you might see as a failure. You don't like to fail."

"Who does?"

"Every time I've failed, I've learned."

He gave a humorless laugh. "Learned not to do it again, or learned how to do it differently?"

"Both." Her gaze was still fastened on his.

Finally he gave up trying to hold on to his romantic past. "I told you my work always got in the way. When I was thirty, I thought settling down might not be a bad idea. But to do it, I'd have to hook up with someone who understood the work. Lois was a public relations expert. We both worked long hours, but mine were longer than hers. I didn't realize how much longer until she told me she was tired of waiting for me to come home every night. In fact, she'd already found someone else to keep her company."

When he saw the softening in Sierra's eyes, he held up his hand. "Don't feel sorry for me. I got over it."

"But you haven't had another serious relationship since."

"That doesn't mean I didn't get over Lois," he said curtly. "It just means that my job was detrimental to our relationship. My work's my life. I've accepted that, and now when I hook up with someone, we meet each other's needs and it's temporary. I don't expect more."

"It's a shame," Sierra said, "that you've never known real love. My parents are deeply in love. They always have been. Anyone can see it when they're together, even after all this time. And when I fell in love with Travis, I was sure I'd love him forever, that he would love me. He would have if he hadn't been killed."

In spite of everything, Ben believed Sierra still had the stars of idealism in her eyes. But that was the difference between twenty-four and thirty-five, he reminded himself. He wasn't so sure she wasn't in love with the idea of being in love rather than the reality. She still had feelings for her dead fiancé, call it love or whatever. He'd been her first and she'd idealized the relationship. How could Ben ever compete with that?

Why should he care? he wondered. He didn't want to compete with her fiancé and he certainly didn't have to.

He was here tonight mending fences with Sierra because they were going to parent together. That's all there was to it.

Yet, as he watched her nibble on a sugar cookie and he ate his, his pulse rate didn't slow down and he still couldn't get one question out of his head. What was she wearing under that robe?

Sierra took a sip of apple juice and eyed him curiously. "What do you do for fun? You have to do something to relax. You can't actually work *all* the time."

"Actually, I can," he said with a wry grin. "But when I get the time, I go down to one of the churches and shoot hoops with the older kids. I've made friends with some of them, and once in a while I take them to the arcade at the mall."

She considered his words, thought about what he'd said. "You're trying to keep them on the straight and narrow?"

"More like give them a role model, encourage them to stay in school, show them they have a future when they think they don't."

She leaned forward and studied him even closer. "You are *not* the tough guy you pretend to be."

Her words threw him. "I don't pretend," he protested.

"You know what I mean, Ben. I get it that you can't be soft in your job, that you have to go after the truth by whatever means you have." She poked a finger gently into his chest. "But in here, you've got a heart as big, if not bigger, than anyone else's."

He absolutely didn't know what to say. He wasn't even sure how she'd come to that conclusion. After all, their interactions hadn't been romantic, tender and full of sweet nothings. She was looking at him as if they had been.

The tip of her finger was a soft pressure on his heart. She smelled of roses again. Her bright eyes were wide open, and he couldn't tell if there was an invitation there or not.

Sierra Girard turned him on. He was almost too old for her, wasn't he? He was definitely too jaded. Yet she was carrying his baby, and God help him, he wanted to take her to bed again. If not that, he wanted to kiss her, needed to kiss her, more than he'd ever thought was possible. He leaned toward her, into the pressure of that finger.

She didn't back away.

As he took her face between his hands, his voice was raspy when he said, "I want to kiss you."

"I want you to kiss me," she agreed softly.

He brought his lips to hers and he thought his heart would jump out of his chest. As their mouths touched, there was no question he was completely aroused. A simple taste wasn't nearly enough and he knew it…knew it from his head to his toes and every place in between. His mind had always ruled his libido. He'd never let desire run rampant, galloping over his good sense…until the engagement party.

His good sense eluded him now, too. Their kiss ignited the hunger he'd felt the first night he'd met her. When his tongue breached her lips, his hand slid from her face and went around her. She held on to him, too, and he could tell from the way she kissed him back, his desire wasn't one-sided. Impatient to feel her body along the length of his, he laid her back on the sofa. Her robe dropped open as his hands slid from her thigh up to her breast. He felt the satin of a short gown. Underneath it, she wore nothing. He palmed her breast, ridged the nipple and she moaned. Were her breasts fuller than he remembered? Would that be happening already?

Just minutes ago, they'd been discussing her dead fiancé and his unfaithful lover. Had sharing their stories led them to think they were sharing intimacy?

He didn't want to let her go. He didn't want to move his body from hers. He didn't want to break the kiss and lever himself up and away. But he *did*...because it was the right thing to do.

She looked befuddled for a moment and sat up, questions in her eyes.

Running his hand down over his face, he shook his head. "Obviously, we're hot together."

Wasn't *that* the understatement of the year! He went on, "We've already made one mistake. We shouldn't compound it. No matter what you think, Sierra, you don't know me and I don't know you. Tell me something. Why did you kiss me back just now?" He needed to know what was going on in her head.

Her cheeks went red. "I wanted to." Suddenly she asked, "You don't think I kissed you to convince you to trust me, do you?"

The truth was, Sierra Girard made his head spin. She seemed innocent, honorable, idealistic. Was she?

She just shook her head. "We *do* have a long way to go, don't we? Maybe I should provide you with references to put in a good word for me." Suddenly, she seemed to realize who he was and what he did. "You've already done a background check on me, haven't you?" She sat up straighter, rebelted her robe and drew the knot together.

"I had to find out if everything you've told me is true," he admitted.

"Camille and Miguel's word weren't enough?"

"Anybody can be fooled, Sierra. We can think we really know someone, then something happens to show us we don't."

"Anyone in particular?" she asked.

"Specifically—Lois. I never expected her to be unfaithful." But not just her. "My brothers, too," he replied. "We've been through a lot together and we think we know one another. My brother Nathan is steadfast, solid, never veers from his course. But last year he put himself into a situation that could have brought him nothing but trouble. He and his wife couldn't conceive. A woman donated her eggs to them. Colleen died in childbirth, and last year, six years later, the woman who donated her eggs turned up in Nathan's life and he invited her right into his house! Something I never thought he'd do."

"Did it work out?" Sierra seemed to be focused on the end result, not the situation itself.

Ben gave her a wry grimace. "He ended up marrying Sara."

"He felt a connection," she mused.

"He wanted to do what was best for his son, so he did the unexpected."

Sierra thought it over. "And your other brother?"

"Sam, who was talking about setting up a veterinary clinic in Haiti one minute, decided to be a sperm donor the next."

"And?"

"And Corrie got pregnant, they married, and they're due soon. That's not the point. Both of them did something I never expected them to do, and I've known them all my life."

"What about *you,* Ben? Will they be surprised that we're—" she hesitated "—that we're pregnant?"

"Nathan was surprised. I haven't heard from Sam yet, or Dad."

"And I'll meet Nathan at Thanksgiving?"

"Yes, you will. Will your aunt be back for the holiday?"

"She hopes to be."

"What does she think about your pregnancy?"

"She…has mixed feelings."

Ironically, Ben understood all too well what *that* meant. "In other words, she's protective of you and she thinks I'm an SOB for *not* protecting you."

Sierra raised her chin. "That's not how I look at it. We had equal responsibility." Her hand went to that knot on her robe again, as if she wanted to make sure it was well and truly fastened.

His body was still thrumming from their kiss, and he wanted to taste her all over again…to carry her to her bedroom. But a physical relationship would muddle what they needed to figure out most.

"We're going to have to discuss child support, whether or not you want to see a lawyer to draw up custody papers."

Sierra shook her head. "That's so…"

"Practical?" he filled in.

She wrinkled her nose. "No. So impersonal. Let's just take this a month at a time. When we get closer to the baby's birth, we can talk about it again."

"I want joint custody, Sierra. I won't settle for less."

She looked worried and troubled and conflicted.

He was conflicted himself and strove to reassure her. "I know an infant needs to be with his or her mother. But I want to be involved in every decision you make."

"You were right to cut off what was happening here," she decided, with sadness tingeing her words. "Until we figure out how to be parents together, anything physical will complicate our lives even more."

Sierra was thinking about what was best for their baby, too. Ben had never been never impulsive or reckless. Yet when he was around Sierra…

His hunger for her was just something he was going to have to deal with, compartmentalize and lock away. Sexual chemistry *would* get in the way of the right decisions and he couldn't let that happen.

He *wouldn't* let that happen.

Chapter Six

Ben's cell phone rang late Monday morning as he exited the courthouse. This was one of those days when his job frustrated him more than satisfied him. Truth be told, there seemed to be more and more of those days.

He'd just negotiated a plea agreement. Another one. He wanted to see the guy get twice the time he was getting, but with full dockets, crowded prisons, more bad guys than they knew what to do with, there was really no choice.

When he checked the number on his phone, he cracked his first real smile of the day. It was his brother Sam.

"What's up?" Ben asked.

"You're an uncle again!" Sam almost shouted. "You're an uncle and I'm a dad, a full-fledged, honest-to-God dad. She was three weeks and a day early, and at first we were worried. But the doc says she's fine. She's five pounds three ounces and the most beautiful baby on earth."

Ben had to laugh. "I'm sure she is. Does the most beautiful baby girl on earth have a name yet?"

"Her name's Diane, after Corrie's mom."

"How's Corrie?"

"She came through it like a trouper. She's exhausted and sleeping right now. Did I tell you Diane has Corrie's hair—red and curly? Corrie insists she has my nose and mouth. It's hard to tell."

Sam was talking so fast, Ben could hardly keep up. "How much caffeine have you had?"

"I don't know, a few hours' worth. I just can't tell you how this feels, Ben. I feel like a giant. I feel like I'm on top of the world. I feel so connected to Corrie. It's like… it's like saying our wedding vows all over again. We made this wonderful little being."

Ben suddenly had the overwhelming yearning to have what Sam had, to have what Nathan had—a wife, a home, a family all of his own.

Sam wound down slowly. "Dad came to see her. He just stood at the nursery window, staring. Nathan, Sara and Kyle are coming later after Corrie gets some rest. I think her doc might even send her home tomorrow. Sara and Nathan are lending Val to us for a couple weeks. With Sara opening her own law practice, she really needs her, but she said Corrie needs her more."

"You're used to Val. She'll be a big help."

"Yeah, she's sort of adopted Corrie along with Sara. The three of them get their hair cut together, go out to lunch, that kind of thing."

"Do you have the house the way you want it yet?"

"Sure do. Except for some of the landscaping. That will have to wait until spring." Sam paused for a moment.

"And speaking of spring and babies…" His brother's silence was an opening for Ben.

"Are you waiting for me to jump in?"

This time Sam chuckled. "Nathan told me you're going to be a dad. What do *you* want to tell me?"

"There's not much to say."

"There could be. What's she like?"

"Sierra is…different. She's only twenty-four and that throws me sometimes."

"A young twenty-four, or an old twenty-four?"

"I don't exactly know how to answer that. In some ways, she seems innocent. In others, she's very mature—she's been all over the world and she lost someone she cared about. I don't think she's playing me, but I've got to make sure. We'll get a DNA test after the baby's born."

"Until then?"

"Until then, I've decided I'm going along with the idea that I'm the father. No harm in that."

Sam was silent.

"What?"

"I know our situations are different, but from the moment Corrie started showing, even before that, really, I knew that little life was in there. I talked to the baby and sang to the baby. I got attached early on. It was a dream in the making and I was part of it."

"But you and Corrie work together. You were friends. When you finally realized you were in love, it wasn't that long after she got pregnant. Our situations are very different."

"Is custody going to be an issue?"

"We're starting to talk about it. Sierra knows I intend to be involved in the child's life. I'm not pushing, though.

She owns a shop on the edge of Old Town so I don't expect she'll run off anywhere. But her parents are in Africa and she has a passport. So I've got to tread lightly, too."

"I know," Sam empathized. "When I thought Corrie was going to move away—it's not even something I wanted to think about. You know that when I wanted her to sign a custody agreement all hell broke loose. But it brought me to my senses."

"As I said, our situation is very different."

"You'll work it out."

Although Sam was younger than Ben and usually came to *him* for advice, Ben knew his brother had been through this situation. He needed his input. "When you had your lawyer draw up that custody agreement, what was that going to mean to you? It wasn't as if you were going to stay home from work to take care of a child on alternate weeks or months."

"No, I wouldn't have done that. But I intended to be at Corrie's at the end of each day to help her put the baby to bed, to find out what happened that day, to solve any problems that cropped up. I wasn't going to not see the baby for a week and then suddenly say—oh, well, this week is my responsibility. Do you know what I mean?"

"Yeah, I do. That's what I've been thinking about. How it's all going to play out."

"A lot depends on this…Sierra and how she feels about you being in the baby's life."

Ben didn't like being the one out of control, but Sam was certainly right. A lot depended on Sierra.

"I have to get back up to the room in case Corrie wakes up. I know I won't see you at Thanksgiving, but do you think you'll get home for Christmas? I want you to get to know your niece."

"I'll make sure I come visit at Christmas. Congratulations, Sam. I'll give Corrie a call later to congratulate her, too."

After a brief goodbye, Ben ended the call. He closed his phone and stared at it as the breeze whipped across him.

His brother was one very lucky man.

Sierra heard her shop bell ring, but she'd decided to spend the afternoon in her small workroom finishing necklaces she wanted to display before the Christmas rush. Her clerk, Olivia, a responsible mom in her thirties, could handle the shop traffic with one hand tied behind her back.

"Ready to take a break?" a chipper female voice asked.

When Sierra looked up from the necklace she was about to crimp, she spotted Camille.

Before she could rise from her chair, her friend was hugging her, practically squealing in delight. "I'm back! We're back. Our honeymoon was wonderful but we couldn't wait to start real life."

Sierra laughed. "It's *all* real life."

Camille leaned away to study her. "How are you?"

Actually, today Sierra was feeling a little…achy, sort of like the way she felt before she got her period. But with her hormones revving up, she expected the sensation to eventually pass. "I'm fine. You've only been gone nine days. Tell me about Aruba."

"Blue skies, blue sea, tropical nights, stars, moon, drinks with umbrellas, lots and lots of time in our room. What else is there to say?"

"Did you get enough of Miguel?" Sierra teased.

"Never. I need a couple of lifetimes with him."

"Is he with you?" Sierra peered through the doorway into the main part of the shop.

"Oh, no. He went to the bank to make sure the place survived without him. Now, tell me about you and Ben. I want every detail."

"He went to my doctor's appointment with me last week. We spent some time together that evening, but I didn't see or hear from him over the weekend."

Camille lounged against Sierra's work counter. "Did you tell him you *want* to see him?"

"No. In fact, it's probably better if we don't see each other—" Sierra felt a twinge in her pelvis different from any she'd experienced that morning. Fear filled her and tightened her throat.

"What's wrong?"

"I don't know. A pain in my side. I'm feeling a little crampy."

"You aren't spotting, are you?"

"I wasn't an hour ago. I'd better check again."

When Sierra stood, the twinge diminished and she felt so relieved. But after she went into the minuscule bathroom, her heart pounded, her ears rung as fear invaded her whole body.

When she exited the cubicle, she said to Camille, "I *am* spotting. Not much, but some." She felt close to tears as she headed for her purse lying on a shelf underneath her work counter. "I've got to call my doctor."

The nurse in Dr. Connor's office directed her, "Come in now. Do you have someone to bring you?"

"Can you take me over?" Sierra asked Camille, knowing she could drive herself if she had to.

"Of course. Come on, grab your jacket and let's go."

A few minutes later in Camille's car with her hands trembling, Sierra made the call she didn't want to make. Taking the business card Ben had given her from her purse, she punched in his cell phone number. Expecting to reach his voice mail, she would just leave a calm message…

He'd obviously checked the caller ID when he answered. "Sierra, I'm on my way to a meeting. Can I call you back?"

She could just say yes and hang up as if this were no big deal. Instead she responded, "I'm on the way to my doctor's. I'm spotting. I just thought you should know. I'll give you a call after I see her."

She heard him swear.

"I know you're busy, Ben. Camille's with me. I'll be fine."

"I'll be there as soon as I can."

In the silence, they held the line open. It was as if they had a lot to say, but didn't know how to say it.

"I'll call you in a little while," she murmured, and then ended the connection.

Camille was watching her.

"He has a meeting, but he said he'll come as soon as he can."

"If that's what Ben said, then he will."

It occurred to Sierra that Camille had known Ben since she'd met Miguel two years ago. "You know him better than I do."

"Time will change that."

Time. But would they have time? If she lost this baby, she'd have no connection to Ben. They'd go back to their separate lives. That made her more sad than she wanted to admit.

Forty-five minutes later, Dr. Connor had finished examining Sierra and performing an ultrasound. Sierra was trying to stay calm, but was failing badly.

When there was a knock on the door, Dr. Connor opened it and Ben stood outside with the nurse.

The nurse told the doctor, "He insisted on coming back."

Dr. Connor glanced at Sierra. "Do you want him here?"

Not only did Ben have every right to be here, but she needed him here. "Yes, it's his baby. He deserves to know what's happening."

After Dr. Connor motioned him inside, Ben crossed to Sierra immediately and took her hand. "Are you okay?"

She nodded, but her fear was so close to the surface she couldn't speak.

"Okay, here's my verdict," the doctor said, giving them both a reassuring smile. "Everything looks fine. Spotting in the first trimester isn't uncommon. As a precautionary measure, I'd like Sierra on bed rest for the next ten days to two weeks. That means feet up, no standing longer than it takes you to go to the bathroom and return to bed again. Do you have someone who can take care of you?"

With her aunt gone, Sierra wasn't sure what to say. Camille might help her out—

"She can stay with me," Ben suddenly responded. "If necessary I'll hire someone to be with her during the day. I'll be there at night."

"Ben! Are you sure? What about your long hours?"

"I can bring work home. We have to do what's best for the baby, Sierra."

She knew he was right. But staying with Ben?

"I'll let the two of you discuss this," the doctor offered, "but I want you going straight somewhere and putting your feet up. No long decisions about packing, carrying suitcases, that kind of thing."

Sierra was really scared now, scared enough to do whatever the doctor ordered.

Dr. Connor studied Ben. "Before you leave, stop at the desk and I'll have a list of home-health-care professionals who can help if you need their services."

After the obstetrician left, Sierra felt shaken, worried and totally out of her element. Staying with Ben seemed so outrageous.

"This is such an imposition," she murmured.

He was still holding her hand, and now he looked directly into her eyes and bent a little closer. "No. It's not an imposition. Taking care of this baby is what we're going to do together. That's what we're doing now."

She'd been trying not to panic, trying to keep all of her emotions in check. But now she felt tears burn in her eyes. "I never expected to be pregnant, but I want this baby, Ben. I really do. I saw her or him when the doctor did the ultrasound."

Releasing her hand, Ben brushed a stray strand of her hair back with the rest.

It was such a tender, gentle gesture, she really felt like crying, and now her eyes did brim with tears.

Ben appeared to be at a loss for a moment, but then his arm went around her and he held her against his chest. "We'll get through this, Sierra. We *will*." Leaning back, tipping her chin up, he smiled. "Do you know how long it's been since I had a roommate?"

"Do I want to know?" she teased back, attempting to be positive. "I don't even know where you live," Sierra said.

"On Comanche Road."

They were talking, trying to have a normal conversation, but his strong arm felt so good around her. His eyes had that intensity that was pure Ben, with a sizzle that could zap her whenever she was close to him. It made her tingle now. He looked as if he wanted to kiss her. Did he?

Suddenly as if he remembered their decision not to become physically involved, he took his arm from around her shoulders. "After you get dressed, I'll take you to my car. Camille is in the waiting room. Do you want me to talk to her about what we're doing?"

"I don't want to impose on her, either. She just got married."

"She's your friend, Sierra. You can just tell her what's happening and go from there."

So that's what they did. After Camille heard what the doctor had ordered, and that Ben insisted that Sierra move in with him, she concurred. "I can take care of you during the day. Miguel will be at work. It's not as if I have anything on my schedule yet."

"Are you sure?" Sierra asked.

"How many times have you taken care of me when I had the flu, or helped me rearrange my apartment or let me whine on your shoulder before Miguel got serious? Of course I want to do this, Sierra."

"Our main problem is what she's going to do to occupy herself," Ben said with a smile.

"I can still design necklaces and bead in bed," Sierra

assured him. “And I have a laptop. I can write e-mails to people I haven’t had time to stay in touch with. I also have an MP3 player and I can read.”

Camille addressed Ben. “I’ll go with you to her aunt’s. I know where she keeps her laptop and everything else.”

“Don’t you have to get back to work?” Sierra asked Ben.

“I want to get you settled first.”

“I don’t know how to thank both of you,” Sierra said gratefully.

“Don’t thank me yet,” Ben teased. “You haven’t tasted my cooking.”

Camille laughed. “There’s always takeout.”

Yes, there was. Maybe this experience wouldn’t be too unsettling for either of them. Maybe all would go well. Just maybe they’d learn how to be parents together.

Just maybe she’d get to know Ben Barclay better than she ever expected to.

Had Sierra actually thought she could be comfortable alone with Ben in his house?

Standing in his living room, his life all around her, she could hardly take it all in. His adobe rancher had three bedrooms. Decorated in Native American patterns and colors, a mixture of sky and earth, mountains and woods, the home had plank flooring and woven rugs, which were backdrops for the lodgepole pine furniture. The table in the dining area near the kitchen overflowed with books and papers and file folders. Photographs of Ben’s family decorated the bookshelves, which held a flat-screen TV and stereo system. The wooden blinds under carved cornices hung at the windows rather than curtains.

What had she expected? Sparse? Glass and chrome? No character to a house where an assistant district attorney spent little time?

Ben motioned her toward a hall where she assumed the bedrooms were located.

There were two doors on the left and one on the right that she suspected led to the master suite.

"I'm going to give you my bedroom," he told her, "because the bathroom's right there. You won't have to walk down the hall."

"I'm not going to put you out of your room!"

"You're going to be spending two weeks in bed, Sierra. I've got a king-size one. You can move around, stretch and have everything at your fingertips." He opened the door into his bedroom. "There's a bookcase headboard so you can set everything there that you need."

"But what are you going to do about your clothes, the things that *you* need?"

"The spare room closet's empty. I'll take clothes over there. As far as the rest..." His eyes glimmered with amusement. "Are you going to lock the door so I can't get in?"

"No, of course not."

"Well, then. There's no need to worry, is there? Come on. Get into bed."

She had to admit that in her dreams she'd imagined being in bed with Ben again, had wondered what his bedroom looked like, had gotten excited over the prospect of him leading her to his bed. But this was so very different than anything she'd dreamed or imagined.

His room was red and gray...and inviting with its down comforter, braided rugs and Minnesota woods prints on the walls. A sweatsuit sprawled over a wooden bedroom chair. The closet door hung open and sneakers lay cock-eyed by the bathroom door.

Ben must have sensed Sierra was feeling totally out of her own world. Crossing to her, he clasped her shoulders, his fingertips lingering on the ends of her hair. "I know you must feel like you've suddenly landed in Oz. Just think of my place as a vacation resort where you can stay in bed and don't have to lift a finger."

"That's not me, Ben."

His thumb soothed her shoulder. "I'm beginning to see that." His voice was low and husky and there was a look in his eyes—

Instead of a kiss on the lips, he kissed her forehead and led her to the bed, his arm around her waist. "Camille will be here in a little while and you'll have everything you need. How about lunch? I don't cook much, but I make a mean omelet."

Giving in to what she and the baby needed, Sierra sat on the bed, pulled his pillows from under the comforter, and stacked them against the headboard. "I'm not very hungry," she admitted, "but I know I have to eat. An omelet sounds good."

As she sat on Ben's bed, looking up at him, realizing that they were going to be together a lot more than she'd ever imagined, her pulse raced faster. He was so handsome in his suit with his tie slightly askew, the top button of his shirt open.

"The truth is, Sierra, I thought about you being in my bed, but not like this. You're safe with me. You know that, don't you?"

"I know." She felt safer with Ben than she had with

anyone. Because he was tall and strong? She didn't think so. It had more to do with the inner man, a sense of integrity that was just part of who he was.

Now seemed like the right time to reach for her purse, open it and slip out the picture of their baby. "The nurse gave this to me after I got dressed. It's what I saw on the screen during the ultrasound. I have a DVD, too, that you can watch when you have time. It's our son or daughter." Her voice thickened as she said the words.

She moved over so Ben could sit on the bed beside her. He did and slowly took the picture from her, just staring at it, totally enthralled. She had been, too. When she'd glimpsed their baby for the first time on the screen, it had filled her with such a sense of joy, she'd felt she could burst. So she knew what Ben was feeling now. At least she hoped that's what he was feeling.

"The arrow is pointing to the baby's head. Do you see it?" she murmured.

"I see it." His voice was husky.

She'd been right about Ben Barclay. He might be as tough as an armadillo on the outside, but he had the kind of heart and depth of character that was hard to find in a man. She'd found it in Travis.

Travis.

If they had gotten married, how soon would they have had children? Would they have come back to the United States? Would Travis have put their child before his work? She knew she would have put their child before anything. She would put *this* child before anything.

"It really is a miracle, isn't it?" Ben's voice was low and gruff. "Everyone says it is, but until a man faces the reality himself—" He shook his head. "I can't even imagine how you feel, having a life growing inside of you."

"This makes it more real," she confessed, reverently touching the picture. "And I imagine when he or she starts moving or kicking, then I'll know for sure."

"Know what?"

"That I'm going to be a mom. I've seen a lot of mothers and babies—women sitting around a communal fire practically naked with babies at their breasts, women who make sure their children are fed before they take a bite of food themselves, women who have walked miles to find their child medical care. I've seen how strong that bond is even though I rarely felt it with my own mother, and I always wondered about it, where it came from, how it happened, how long it lasted. I know for me, the bond's going to last a lifetime, a cord that's never going to be cut, at least not on my side."

"Uh-oh. I can see a teenage rebellion in the works," Ben teased.

She smiled. "I know I'll have to let go eventually, but that cord…I'm going to hold on tight to it." Emotion got the best of her again and her voice broke when she said, "I can't lose this baby, Ben."

"We'll do everything in our power to keep you and the baby healthy and safe. That's why you're going to let me and Camille wait on you, right?"

The doorbell rang, and a second later Ben's cell phone beeped. He checked the number and answered it on the way to the door.

Sierra could hear Camille's cheery "Here I am."

She listened as Ben told the phone caller, "Hold on a minute."

He directed Camille, "Put everything wherever she needs it."

When Camille entered the bedroom, her arms full of clothes, she said to Sierra, "I'm going to make room for these in his closet. I brought you mainly lounging stuff and sweats. I didn't think you'd need much else."

Camille was inside Ben's walk-in closet when he returned to the room.

He called, "Camille?"

She poked her head out.

"I need to get back to my office. Should I stir up an omelet or can you manage something?"

Camille wrinkled her nose at him. "In spite of rumors to the contrary, I'm quite capable in the kitchen."

Ben gave her a sly smile.

"Okay, Miguel told you about the overdone roast and the scorched refried beans, but I really *can* handle a few eggs."

"I'll take your word for it."

"Will you get lunch?" Sierra asked him.

"I'll get something eventually." He glanced at Camille. "I'll try to be home by six. Is that okay for you?"

"It's fine. Miguel never ends his workday much before seven."

"Hel-lo," Sierra interrupted them. "I'm here. If there's an hour or two between shifts, don't worry. I'm not going to do anything I shouldn't."

Ben and Camille exchanged a look.

"Really," Sierra vowed. She touched the picture in her lap. "I mean it, Ben."

He nodded as if he finally did believe her. Crossing to the bed, he studied her with an intensity that seemed more intimate than a kiss.

Moments later, he was gone.

"I'll bet he skips lunch more often than he eats it," Sierra murmured.

"And you care about that?" Camille asked.

Since Camille was her very best friend, because Sierra knew she had to be honest with herself, she replied, "I think I care too much."

Chapter Seven

Late that night, Ben stood outside of Sierra's bedroom door and didn't know whether to knock. He'd moved his work clothes over to the spare bedroom earlier, but not his sweats, and he really needed to go for a run tomorrow morning. So it was either disturb Sierra now, or wait until morning before the sun came up.

He knocked.

When she didn't answer right away, he thought she might be asleep, but then he heard a muffled "Come in." It didn't sound like Sierra at all.

They'd had an unremarkable evening. He'd looked in on her now and then, but mostly he'd worked at the dining-room table. When he'd gone to check on her the next time, her light had been out.

The door was already open a few inches and he pushed

it wider. "I'm sorry if I woke you. I want to take a run in the morning and I need some clothes."

When there was no answer, he finally moved his gaze to the bed. He'd been avoiding doing it. He really didn't need to see Sierra in one of those tempting little nightgowns.

After he switched on the wrought-iron lamp on the dresser and its dim glow reached the bed, he crossed to Sierra so he could see her face. She was propped on two pillows, her laptop beside her. As he drew closer, he could see her nose was red. From crying?

"What's wrong? Aren't you feeling well?"

"I'm feeling okay. Frustrated thinking about at least ten days of this, but okay. The spotting has stopped."

Her hand was in a fist, a tissue crunched inside. He tapped his finger on her thumb. "Then what's this?"

"It's nothing for you to be concerned about, Ben."

All right, so he was a lawyer, and when somebody said something like that, he, of course, couldn't let it be. "Are you thinking about whether or not you might lose the baby?"

"Sure. But mostly I'm trying to be positive. I just… couldn't get to sleep right away so I checked my e-mail. I received a letter from my parents—my mom. But as I said, it's nothing you have to be concerned about."

He moved her laptop and sat on the bed. "If something stresses you out, that's not good for the baby. Stress isn't good for you. So, yes, your e-mail is my concern. Did you tell your parents you're pregnant and they're appalled by the idea?"

"No, nothing as serious as that. They're not coming back to the States for Thanksgiving. I was so hoping they would and I could tell them about the baby in person. But I should have known better than to hope for that."

"What if you asked them to come back?"

"Our relationship isn't like that, Ben. I learned a long time ago that just because I needed something from them doesn't mean they can give it to me."

"But aren't you going to give them the chance?"

He knew the answer as soon as he asked the question. It was obvious Sierra had been rejected by her parents over and over again in all the little ways that mattered.

"Do your parents know about your life here?" he asked.

"Do they know I own a shop and I'm living with my aunt? Sure. They know I make jewelry, but I don't think they have any idea what it means to me, to create, design and sell it. They haven't been back here for three years so they've never seen the shop."

"You haven't seen them for three years?"

"Summer, a year ago, I flew to London to meet them while they took a few weeks' R & R."

Her voice quivered slightly, and Ben had the urge to pull her to him and cuddle her close. But he fought it, distracting himself with the rose scent in the room. Earlier, he'd noticed a dish of dried petals on the dresser that Camille must have brought from Sierra's bedroom at her aunt's. Studying Sierra in the humongous bed now, he noticed not only her outward beauty, but her sweetness, which had been so lacking in many of the women he'd dated. She was making a valiant effort to be upbeat, to take everything in stride, including being alone here with him.

"With parents like you had, why aren't you all messed up, afraid of your own shadow, afraid to reach out and hesitant to look to anyone for support?" he asked, curious.

"Your mom left you. Why aren't *you* messed up?" she returned, her voice strong again.

"Because I always had my dad and my brothers."

"And I always had my aunt. Sometimes she was thousands of miles away, but I always knew she was there. That mattered so much. When I went to high school, I met Camille. We clicked and knew we'd always be best friends."

Ben so wanted to reach out and kiss her again. But under the circumstances, that would be a mistake.

What if they *did* lose their baby?

He was truly beginning to believe this baby was his. Sierra didn't have the artifice to pull off deception. Taking her hand in his, he intertwined their fingers. "I know it's not the same thing at all, but you're welcome to share my family."

"I'd like that," she admitted. "My aunt will be home soon. I can't speak for her, but it would be great if we could all have Thanksgiving together."

"You'd better not volunteer her before you talk to her."

"She can be blunt, and annoyingly forthright sometimes, but I think she'll like the idea of a lot of people around the table at Thanksgiving. That's the way it should be."

Sierra had so many qualities he'd never really looked for in a woman—an eye on something deeper than a career, an outlook that made the best of whatever she had to face, a vulnerability that came from being her own person at a young age.

The intimacy of the shadowed room, the attraction he'd felt for her from the first moment he'd seen her, the slip of moonlight drifting in urged him to lean close and touch his lips to hers. She gave a startled little gasp and her hands went to his shoulders, not to push him away, but to bring him closer.

But before the kiss could get out of hand, he put on the brakes, leaned away and got to his feet.

She didn't say anything and neither did he.

What was there to say? He hadn't been looking for a relationship. He didn't know if he could ever trust a woman again. Sierra still wasn't over her first love. Between them, they had a lot of baggage. They wouldn't be here together tonight if it weren't for her pregnancy and the chance she might lose the baby. There was nothing permanent about this situation.

He went to the dresser and opened a drawer.

"Ben," she called softly.

He knew her parents' e-mail had upset her. He didn't want to upset her more. "It's late, Sierra. Let's just table everything until tomorrow."

He stacked his clothes in his arms and added his sneakers to the top of the pile. "I'll be out at first light and back before you know I'm gone. I'll take my cell phone. Are you okay with that?"

"Yes. Camille said she'd be here about eight, so if you need to leave before that, don't worry about it."

They'd both be bending over backward while she stayed with him. That's because they were still strangers who didn't know each other well enough to be comfortable. Maybe by the end of two weeks…

Nope. Two weeks wasn't enough time to get to know a person. He and Sierra really had little in common, and that would become more obvious rather than less so as time went on. But for now, he would do whatever he had to do for the well-being of their baby. For now, he'd try to be a good host, and he damn well better stop kissing her or he'd learn for sure what trouble really meant.

* * *

The sky had just started to lighten when Sierra heard Ben's cell phone beep in his room across the hall. She'd slept fitfully, thinking about the kiss and everything she and Ben had talked about, thinking how close she felt to him sometimes, how far away at others.

Five minutes later, Ben knocked, then came into her room. He saw her sitting up in bed. "My phone wake you?"

He was already dressed, not in running gear, but in a suit and tie. "Yes, but I wasn't exactly sleeping. Were you called into work?"

"Not exactly. One of the teenagers I befriended down at the church has a friend who's in trouble. He was a lookout for an attempted robbery. Diego wants me to see if I can help him. His friend doesn't have any other strikes against him, so I thought I'd try. Are you okay with me leaving now? I don't want you to feel you won't have anybody here if you need someone."

"I'm feeling good. Camille will be here soon."

"Promise me you won't get up until she arrives."

"Ben—"

"Sierra, I mean it. It's the only way I'll leave."

It was obvious he was torn by all his responsibilities, which now included her. "I promise."

He was standing about a foot from the bed and not coming any closer. Even at that distance, she could feel the current between them and wondered if he could, too.

Clearing her throat, she asked, "So what do you think you can do to help this boy?"

"I'll be there in an unofficial capacity unless the case lands on my desk. He didn't have a weapon, and as I said, he hasn't been in trouble before. That's all in his favor."

"But you're really going because of—"

He filled in the name. "Diego."

"Are you afraid he's involved?"

"My guess is he knew what was going to go down, maybe not when, but he knew. I'll see that he gets home safe and give him another pep talk so he doesn't end up in his friend's shoes."

She was struck again by how much Ben cared, the same way Travis had cared for men, women and children who couldn't get help with the simplest of diseases. Ben really didn't have time in his life for her, and maybe not even for their baby, whether he realized it or not. That was the best reason why their relationship should stay platonic while she spent this time with him. After that, she'd worry about what came next.

A week later, Ben was sitting in his bedroom with Sierra, digging into a carton of General Tso's chicken and trying to keep his gaze away from her pretty face when the doorbell rang.

Sierra wound a lo mein noodle around her fork and asked, "Are you expecting someone?"

"Not that I know of." He set his meal on the dresser and went to answer the door. When he opened it, he found a woman, about five-eight, in jeans and a colorful poncho. Her gray hair was cut in a no-nonsense, chin-length style and her dark brown eyes stared straight into his.

"Are you Ben Barclay?" she asked in a clipped but not unfriendly tone.

"Yes, I am. And you are?"

"I'm Gina Ruiz, Sierra's aunt. I've come to take her home."

Ben absorbed the woman's words, not liking the empty feeling they gave him. Usually he analyzed a situation, debated the pros and cons, then made a conclusion. He never just blurted out his opinion. This time he did. "I don't think that would be advisable. She's supposed to be on bed rest. She only has four days to go and it doesn't seem like a practical, good thing to disrupt it at this point."

Gina tilted her head and studied him more thoroughly. "Can I see her?"

"Of course you can. Come on in. She's down the hall to the right."

Sierra's aunt's stride was quick and graceful, much like Sierra's. She didn't hesitate, but walked right into Ben's bedroom.

He heard Sierra's joyful "Aunt Gina! You're not supposed to be home for another week."

Ben stepped into the room as Sierra's aunt sat down on the bed to hug her. "I decided to cut my trip short. I was just telling Mr. Barclay I'd planned to take you home with me." She glanced over her shoulder at him. "He seems to think that will disrupt your doctor's orders."

Sierra looked from Ben to her aunt and he knew what she was thinking. She was thinking she was a burden to him, a responsibility he didn't want, that she should go with her aunt if it would make life easier for him.

He vetoed the idea before Sierra could even consider it. "The doctor told you you shouldn't get up except to go to the bathroom. If you go home now, then you'll have the trip home, you'll have to gather your things, and once you're there, at your own place, will you stay in bed like you're supposed to? We have a routine set up, Sierra. I don't think you should change it until your doctor's appointment on Friday. Then if she says all systems are go, it won't be an issue."

It was obvious that Sierra also didn't want to hurt her aunt. "I'd love to come home with you, Aunt Gina, but I do think Ben's right." When she saw her aunt's disappointment, she added, "But I think Camille might need a break. You could keep me company during the day and she could go back to being a newlywed."

Gina thought that over. "Do you have Camille's phone number? I can call her and work something out." She nodded to the containers of Chinese food. "While you two finish supper."

Sierra flipped her cell phone open, brought up Camille's number and handed the phone to her aunt.

Gina stepped outside the bedroom to make the call. Ben heard her footsteps down the hall and into his living room.

"She's all-business, isn't she?" he said in a low voice.

"That's Aunt Gina. She's a get-the-job-done kind of person." Sierra looked down at her papers and laptop and bead board on the side of the bed, then her gaze met Ben's. "Are you sure you want me to stay? I really do feel fine. A trip home in the car shouldn't hurt anything."

When she looked at him like that, her eyes big and vulnerable, he couldn't stay away from her. He went to the bed and sat down beside her. "I think we should stick with our plan. It's worked so far and you haven't disrupted my life. I know you're probably bored in here while I work most nights."

"I can always find something to do. You're within yelling distance. It's nice to know someone's out there. I'm not here for you to entertain me. I'm here so I don't lose this baby."

On that, they were in one-hundred-percent agreement.

A few minutes later, Gina slipped back into the room, her poncho gone now. Her red cotton blouse was crisp, without a wrinkle. "Camille was agreeable to my idea. I'll be coming over to make you breakfast and stay with you throughout the day. As a bonus, I'll even make supper. That way Ben won't have to worry about it. Is that all right with you, Ben? I can call you Ben, can't I?"

"Ben is fine, Ms. Ruiz."

"Gina's good for me. We'll get to know each other this way." She patted Sierra's hand. "After all, we're all going to be involved in this baby's life. We might as well figure out how to get along."

Ben wondered exactly what Sierra had told her aunt about the engagement party, about getting pregnant, about staying with him now. But Gina Ruiz was giving nothing away. She was just stating the obvious and he respected her for that. He wasn't sure she approved of him or of Sierra staying with him. That bothered him. It had been a very long time since he'd wanted anyone's approval.

After Gina stood, she collected the cartons of Chinese food. "I disrupted your supper. I'll take this out to the microwave and warm it up. Then you can start all over again."

"If you'd like to join us…" Ben offered.

"Oh, no. I ate before I came over. I'll just sit with you so we can get that awkward first conversation out of the way. Then I'll leave you to your evening." She swept out of the room, their food in hand.

Ben didn't know whether to laugh or to wish Gina Ruiz gone.

"She takes some getting used to," Sierra admitted, "but once you get to know her, I think you'll like her."

"Can she cook?" he teased.

"Sure can. She makes an egg-and-salsa casserole that's to die for. Her steak and peppers is great, too, not to mention her quesadillas. You just might be glad she came home early. We won't disrupt your life, Ben, I promise."

Ben knew Sierra's words were heartfelt. The thing was—she had already disrupted his life and he was trying to get used to the idea that it would never be the same again.

On Friday morning, the press conference for the Children's Art Project had proceeded according to schedule, but Ben was glad it was over. This endeavor, a legacy from a former district attorney, was worthwhile. The project spotlighted children's talent and showed what they were feeling and thinking about what was going on in the city around them. But Ben had stood to the rear of the crowd waiting for his phone to vibrate, waiting for Sierra's call after her doctor's appointment.

From across the crowded room, he suddenly spied a man trying to get his attention. Ben knew who he was, a defense attorney from one of the large partnerships in town. They'd been opponents more than a few times in the courtroom, but maintained a civil relationship because they respected each other. Cord Whitmore was a few years older than Ben, his own height, with green eyes that were sharp and intelligent.

Cord finally got within shouting distance. "Can we talk?"

They both angled toward a corner where they'd have a modicum of quiet.

Cord started off, "I was going to make an appointment with you, but this will do."

"About a case?" Ben was surprised Cord would want to talk in a public arena.

"No, not this time. I've become involved in a project you might like." He held his hand up before Ben could say anything. "This isn't something after hours that will take more of your time."

"What kind of project?" Ben asked warily. After all, he was a prosecutor and Cord was a defense attorney.

"I suppose you heard that John Alvarez passed away last month?"

John Alvarez had been a prominent businessman in the Albuquerque area, was wealthy beyond most men's dreams and had lived to a ripe old age of eighty-seven. There had been a few articles in the paper about his passing and his life.

"Yes, I knew," Ben replied.

"Well, it turns out he left an endowment. With this money we're supposed to set up a law firm that would specialize in juvenile cases—kids who get in trouble for the first time and can't afford good representation. We're searching for the right person to head it up. We have a list of possibilities, but I believe you're the most qualified and you're an attorney who would be the most interested in helping kids. I know a few you've kept from joining gangs."

"I'm a prosecutor, Cord."

"Yeah, and a damn good one. If you filled a spot like this, you'd actually have time for each case and the opportunity to seek out remedial action for a first-time offender. Isn't that the kind of work you might want to do instead of constantly settling for plea agreements that eat at you because you know justice isn't being served?"

Cord had gotten to the crux of what Ben disliked most about his job. He'd been a prosecutor for nine years now. Did he really want to think about changing his focus?

"You have time to think about it," Cord told him. "We're just in the preliminary stages of setting this up. I know you wouldn't have any trouble securing the position of head counsel if you wanted it."

"Who makes the decision?"

"Alvarez named five people to a board—his son, who owns businesses all over the state, a retired judge, two retired schoolteachers and a college professor who teaches ethics. They'll make the final decision on who's hired. My recommendation will go a long way. Besides that, they know the kind of work you do. Will you seriously consider it?"

Ben turned the idea of this kind of work over in his head. "I'll seriously consider it."

In his trousers' pocket, Ben's phone vibrated. He slipped his hand in and pulled it out. To Cord he said, "I've got to take this call."

Cord nodded. "I'll be in touch. If you have any questions, call me."

As Cord moved away, Ben inched closer to the wall and jammed a finger in one ear so he could hear Sierra better.

"Ben?" Sierra asked. "Is this a bad time?"

"No, this is fine. What did the doctor say?" Ben couldn't believe there was a lump in his throat that felt like it could choke him. What if the bed rest hadn't helped? What if she lost this baby, after all?

"Everything's fine, Ben. The doctor said it all looks good. The baby's growing as it should. She advised me to still go easy next week, not work twelve-hour days or anything like that. But then the pregnancy should proceed normally."

Ben felt relief, such relief he felt ten pounds lighter.

Sierra went on, "So Aunt Gina is going to help me gather my things and go home. I'll be out of your hair and you don't have to worry about supper tonight, or what time you get home."

The idea of going back to his house without her being there filled him with a kind of hollowness he'd never experienced before. It was crazy.

Inside him a question rose up. *What's next?* But he really couldn't ask Sierra that. After all, he had his work, she had her shop, and the baby wouldn't be born for another seven months. So what was there to say?

"Ben?"

"Yes?"

"I want to thank you for everything. I really appreciate you giving up your life for the past week and a half. I'm sure I could have managed, but you made me feel protected and safe. That helped when I was worried I would lose the baby."

That lump was back and he didn't know how to get rid of it. He didn't even know what to answer her. So he said, "No thanks necessary."

She didn't respond to his comment. She seemed to be waiting for him to say something else. But he wasn't sure what the next step was or where they should go from here. So he simply asked, "Stay in touch, will you?"

"I will."

When Ben closed his phone, he didn't like ending the connection. He didn't like not knowing what Sierra would be doing and who she'd be doing it with.

You have separate lives, he reminded himself. But his reminder gave him no solace at all.

Chapter Eight

The drive to White Rock Overlook always filled Sierra with a sense of anticipation and expectation. The point near Los Alamos looked over a grand vista with a waterfall and gorge. Today, going there with Ben, she wasn't exactly sure what she felt.

She glanced over at him. It had been two weeks since she'd left his house…two weeks since she'd heard from him…two weeks of wondering what he was thinking and feeling. She knew he was embroiled in preparation for a trial along with all of his other cases, and maybe she—and their baby—hadn't been a consideration at all. But when he called last night and asked her to take a drive with him, she wondered if maybe he'd missed her as she'd missed him.

The beauty of the russet cliffs, the cerulean sky and puffy clouds could distract her from the fact that she'd fallen for Ben, big time. Mistake or not, her heart was tied up with more than their baby.

After they parked, Ben came around the car and helped her down from the SUV. She felt as if she could almost see the world as it had once been thousands of years ago—the scene was primal, elemental and heart-stopping. For some reason, she was particularly aware of the life growing inside of her and Ben standing beside her.

"Let's walk over to the edge," Ben suggested, his arm going around her, his hand settling at her waist. She felt a sense of rightness about that, yet some trepidation, too. They'd fallen into this situation like the proverbial two stars that had collided.

The breeze tossed her hair and buffeted her suede jacket. In mid-November, winter had come to the area. Ben's cable-knit sweater made her want to burrow into his chest and just hold on to him.

At the edge, amid scruffy piñon pines and sage, they faced the faraway waterfall.

"I know you said Sandia Peak was one of your favorite places. But the road's icy and I wasn't sure how the altitude would affect you—being pregnant and all. This is one of *my* favorite top-of-the-world places."

"It's beautiful up here." She could almost believe they were looking down at the Garden of Eden.

"I have something to ask you."

Ben's voice was husky and her heart pounded against her chest. Was he going to bring up joint custody again? All the conditions they needed to work out? Would he want notarized guarantees and promises? Had he thought that by bringing her here they could both consider their situation with more perspective?

"What do you want to ask me?" She studied him, searching his face for a hint of what was on his mind.

"I've put a lot of thought into our situation."

"And?" she prompted.

"And...I want to be an everyday dad, not a weekend one."

Taking a deep breath, she reminded herself not to panic. But if he wanted custody—

"I don't want our son or daughter to be born illegitimate," he went on. "I don't want you to meet someone else, marry him and give my baby a stepdad. There's only one way to secure being a family unit, and that's if we get married. Will you marry me, Sierra?"

The question wrapped around her with the wind. She held no illusions that Ben loved her. He might be attracted to her, but this question had everything to do with their child rather than her. If she hadn't gotten pregnant, they wouldn't even be standing here.

In an instant her engagement to Travis and everything that had happened rushed through her. She'd loved Travis, but she was also falling in love with Ben. She and Travis might have lived a vagabond life, and she really hadn't thought about the repercussions of that. She'd been young, idealistic.

Now...

Now Ben was asking her to look at the practical side of everything. One truth stood out. As Ben's wife and his child's mother, she could put down permanent roots. She could have the family she'd always dreamed of. As her love for Ben grew, surely he would come to care for her, too. They *did* have chemistry to build on, as well as the best interests of their baby.

Her silence didn't make him impatient. "I understand if you need time to think about this."

Searching Ben's face, she found strength and determination with just a hint of uncertainty. Marriage. It was a big step and she realized he wasn't sure about it, either.

But suddenly she *was* sure, more sure than she'd been about anything in a long time. "I don't need time to think about it. I want our son or daughter to have a mom and dad. The best way for that to happen is for us to be together."

She thought he might take her into his arms. She thought he might even kiss her.

Yet he didn't. He simply looked relieved. "We can go to the justice of the peace."

Actually, she'd like a church wedding, but…she could see the practicality of what Ben was suggesting. "You don't want to wait until your family flies in for Thanksgiving?" The holiday was less than two weeks away.

"No. I want this to be a fait accompli by then. We can get married Monday. I don't have to be in the courtroom. We can be all settled in by Thanksgiving."

He just wanted to get it over with. She wanted…more. But she also wanted their lives on a manageable course, both of them knowing what to expect.

He rested his hand on her shoulder. "You won't be sorry, Sierra. I'll take care of you and the baby. We'll have a good life."

She had so many questions…so many what-ifs. Truth be told, so many doubts, too. Underlining all of it, she wanted her hand in Ben's, with both of them looking in the same direction.

She reached up and covered his hand with hers. "I'll call Camille and Miguel and we can plan our wedding."

"How do you think your aunt will feel about this?" Ben asked.

Sierra squeezed Ben's hand. "Let's go find out."

Standing in the justice of the peace's living room late Monday afternoon, Sierra tried to forget that he wasn't a man of God, tried to wipe out the pictures of the church she'd rather be married in, tried to reconcile this wedding with the one she'd always imagined.

She had chosen her dress from her closet with care. It had the colors of a New Mexican sunset, pink and peach with a bit of sky thrown in. She'd caught Ben glancing at her often, hoping he found her attractive on their wedding day, even though she wasn't in a traditional gown.

Camille stood at her elbow, holding a small white bouquet that had come with the justice of the peace's package for the wedding. Ben had made all of the arrangements and yesterday had taken her shopping for wedding rings. They'd bought simple gold bands.

Sierra was aware of her aunt's presence, too. Aunt Gina sat in a folding chair looking on. Her response to Sierra and Ben's announcement that they were going to marry hadn't been a jubilant one. In fact, she'd pinned Ben with a glare and asked, "Are you sure you want to do this?" He hadn't hesitated an instant in his response that he absolutely did. Not reassured, even up until this morning, her aunt had counseled Sierra, "You can still back out. This isn't a done deal."

To Sierra it was. She'd made a decision and there was no turning back. She and Ben would make this marriage work for the sake of their child.

And what about you? a little voice whispered as Ben slipped the wedding band on her finger.

I'm going to be the wife he needs and a good mother to his child.

Ben hadn't mentioned the paternity test again, and Sierra hoped that he'd come to trust her the same way she trusted him.

At the end of the ceremony, the justice of the peace smiled at them. "I now pronounce you husband and wife. If you'd like to kiss, that's fine with me."

Whether for the on-lookers or for themselves, Ben wrapped his arms around her. In his embrace, Sierra was hopeful about their future. When his head bowed and his lips sealed to hers, the living room and everyone but her and Ben dropped away. She only hoped he could feel their connection, too. As his tongue dipped into her mouth and she responded with greedy hunger, she realized she could never have married him if she didn't love him. She *did* love him. It was a new love, somewhat based on the potent chemistry between them. But there was more to it, too. She knew she wanted to explore everything about Ben, meet his needs and have him meet hers, find a future with him and one for their child.

The justice of the peace cleared his throat loudly. The sound penetrated Sierra's haze, and the profound silence that followed it penetrated, too. She could feel the exact instant Ben decided to stop the kiss. She wanted to protest yet knew she couldn't. After all, they weren't alone. They weren't in a private place. They were at their wedding ceremony and her aunt was watching.

When Ben pulled away, Sierra knew she should feel embarrassed, but she didn't. Her aunt was giving her a curious look, and Sierra pulled herself together as Ben leaned away. She stepped back and Camille handed her her bouquet.

"I have papers for you to sign," the justice of the peace said. "Then you can celebrate."

"Yes, we can," Aunt Gina agreed, her gaze now going to Ben. "The caterer is setting up everything at the house as we speak. I wanted to surprise you. They even promised me a wedding cake, so *something* about the wedding will be a little bit traditional." Her words seemed to challenge Ben to contradict her.

His shoulders went straight and his back stiff, but his words were polite. "Thank you, Gina. Sierra and I didn't expect anything like that."

Sierra gave her aunt a huge hug. "You always know just what to do to make everything right."

"I wish that were true," her aunt replied, looking from Ben to Sierra. "I do wish that were true."

A half hour later, they were sharing a light supper in her aunt's living room. Ben sat beside Sierra on the sofa, quiet. Although Camille and Miguel kept the conversation flowing, it still lagged now and then.

When Ben's cell phone rang, Sierra was afraid he'd be called away to work. But when he checked the number, he smiled. Putting the phone to his ear, he said, "Dad?" Then he listened. After a few moments, he passed the phone to Sierra. "It's my father. He'd like to speak to you."

Everyone in the room was quiet, and Sierra didn't know if she should find a private corner or not. But she decided just to take the call right there. "Hello?" she asked tentatively.

"Sierra? This is Galen Barclay."

"Hello, Mr. Barclay."

"How about if you call me Galen."

"All right…Galen."

"I know this is probably awkward for you and we'll have to get to know each other eventually. But I just wanted to welcome you into the family. You're a Barclay now, and that means something."

Tears came to her eyes. "Thank you."

"No thanks necessary. Family is important. You'll know that for sure when you meet all of us. I didn't want to interrupt anything, but I just wanted you to know I'm looking forward to getting to know you."

"I'm looking forward to getting to know you, too," she responded. "My parents are very far away most of the time and we're not…close."

"Well, that's a shame. Maybe we can take up the slack. Now, you take care of yourself, you hear?"

"I will."

Galen said goodbye, and she handed the phone back to Ben. After a final comment or two to his dad, he clicked the phone shut.

Sierra sought her aunt's gaze. "He wanted to welcome me into the family."

Gina cocked her head. "That was generous of him. Now, why don't we cut that wedding cake?"

After enjoying slices of the small, three-tiered cake decorated with real roses and greenery, Camille and Miguel kissed and hugged Ben and Sierra, then left.

"Are you tired, honey?" Gina asked her niece.

"A little, but it's a good tired."

"Why don't you wrap up a layer of that cake to take along."

As Sierra went to the kitchen to do as her aunt suggested, she watched Gina take Ben aside to have a quiet conversation with him. Sierra wondered what that was all about. She found out as soon as she and Ben climbed into the SUV to drive home.

Home. Could she really start to think of Ben's house as home?

In the car, she felt Ben's tension and wasn't sure what it meant. "What did my aunt want to talk to you about?"

Ben didn't answer her right away. He glanced at her and then set his eyes back on the road ahead of him. When they stopped for a traffic light, his words were measured and careful. "Your aunt is concerned about you."

That was a diplomatic answer if she ever heard one. "I'm your wife now, Ben. I want to know the truth. Aunt Gina can be overprotective sometimes."

"She doesn't believe we should have gotten married."

"I know."

"You know?"

"She tried to talk me out of it. She told me I should just move in with you, not marry you. That way, if we didn't stay together, we wouldn't have so much to untangle."

"You're kidding."

"No. I told you Aunt Gina is always blunt. She says what she thinks. But at least I don't have to guess." She tried to make the conversation lighter than it was, because obviously her aunt's opinion bothered Ben.

"She thinks I married you to have control over you and our child," Ben informed her, frustration edging his tone. "That's the word she used—*control.* That's not what this is about, Sierra."

Sierra wasn't sure what their marriage was about yet. She believed Ben was trying to do the right thing, that he was raised to do the right thing. That meant taking responsibility. But duty and responsibility were very different from what she wanted in this relationship.

"Do you believe me?" he asked her.

"I believe that you think two parents would be better for our baby. Two parents who are around twenty-four hours a day."

"That's right, and that isn't control."

"I know. Aunt Gina will understand when she gets to know you better. She's…she's divorced."

"She was married?"

"Long ago, when she was in her twenties. It was a whirlwind romance and she was…deceived. He was charming and flattering and wonderful before they were married. Afterward, he became abusive. Within six months, she filed for a protective order and divorce. The experience really changed her, made her less trusting, more analytical. She doesn't want me to end up in a situation anything like that one."

"She doesn't trust your judgment?"

"She *has* to trust my judgment. I'm married to you now. That's just the way it's going to be. She'll come around, Ben, once we spend more time around her."

Silence lay heavy between them until Sierra offered, "It was nice of your dad to call and talk to me."

"Dad's a tough old bird sometimes, but he means well. He wants me to take you home for Christmas."

"Do you want to go back to Rapid Creek for Christmas?"

"If the flight's okay with your doctor and you're feeling good."

"I'll talk to her about it at my next appointment."

A few minutes later, Ben pulled into his carport and

switched off the ignition. He was out of the SUV and around to Sierra's side before she unfastened her seat belt. After he opened her door, he extended his hand to her.

Dusk had fallen, but a motion-detector light had gone on when Ben neared the side door. It illuminated his face. His expression was hard to read, but she thought she saw a hint of unsureness there. They were both uncertain of what came next.

Taking his proffered hand, she stepped down, took a few steps toward the doorway, and then stopped. There was a box sitting on the step.

When Sierra bent to pick it up, Ben commanded sharply, "Don't!"

She looked up at him. "Ben?"

"Don't touch it," he repeated, circling her waist and guiding her to the far corner of the carport. "Just stay there. I'm going to make a call."

"Tell me what this is about."

"I don't know what's in that box and I'm not taking any chances. Then we'll talk about it."

A half hour later there were two patrol cars in the driveway. The box was gone, taken away in a van. Sierra was sitting in Ben's SUV again, waiting. Finally, Ben said goodbye to the officers, came to fetch her and led her into the house.

"What was it?" she asked him.

He really appeared to be debating with himself whether he should tell her or not.

"I want to know," she pressed.

"It was a prank."

"*What* was in the box?"

He raked his hand through his hair. "It was a dead rat."

After she absorbed that, she asked, "Who left it?"

"They're checking it for prints."

"This has something to do with your upcoming trial?" she guessed.

"Possibly."

"Ben, be straight with me."

"All right," he admitted, blowing out a sigh of frustration. "It was probably another warning from the brother of the man I'm going to convict. I'll have a security system company here tomorrow morning to put an alarm on the house. Trials bring out the worst in people."

"You're in danger, aren't you?"

"No, I'm not." After he crossed to her, he rested his hands at her waist. "I don't know how to explain this to you, Sierra. I know I've said it before, but that box is just part of the territory."

The territory she'd stepped into today by marrying him. She'd known she was putting her heart in jeopardy because Ben guarded himself so carefully. But now there seemed to be double jeopardy.

He read her thoughts. "Do you want to undo what we just did? Have our marriage annulled?"

Did she? Did she want to love Ben knowing she could lose him? They didn't even know what kind of life they could have together yet. She didn't know how much she was going to see him, when they'd be together, if they were going to run their lives separately. Did he truly want to be married, or was custody of their child his only reason for saying "I do"?

It was time she faced the reality of marrying him. "I don't want to undo it, but I do want to know what you expect of me."

Without hesitation, he shook his head. "I don't have any expectations. We're not in the usual situation. We're just going to have to take this day by day and see what develops."

She glanced down the hall toward his bedroom. "Are we going to sleep together?"

Now he slid his hands under her hair. The feel of his fingertips against her skin made her heart jump crazily. "The question is," he drawled slowly, "do you *want* to share my bed with me? I know the doctor said that your pregnancy's on track, but I don't want to do anything that would put you or the baby at risk. So, yes, I'd like you to share my bed, but as far as sex goes, we'll give it some time."

How much time? a little voice inside her head wanted to know. But she didn't ask the question aloud.

Suddenly Ben released her and took a step back. "So, should I put all those clothes in the SUV in the spare room or in *my* room?"

This was her wedding night. She wasn't going to spend it separated from her husband. "In your room."

His mouth turned up slightly at the corners and he looked pleased. "Why don't you get comfortable. After I unload everything, we'll have a second piece of wedding cake."

As Ben exited the house, she watched him stop and look down at the step where the box had been. He checked up and down the street before he finally went to the SUV.

Just how much danger was her husband in?

Torture. It was pure torture lying in the same bed with Sierra and not touching her. Yes, this had been his idea, and what a stupid one!

He was married. His wife was across the bed and he wasn't reaching for her. Because he was afraid he'd hurt her? Hurt the baby? Or was his concern more than physical? Was it as deep as the problems they might have if they became really intimate? So many questions rolled through his head. Had they made a mistake? How drastically was his life going to change? What expectations did Sierra have of him? Or he of her?

The wind had picked up outside. A cold front was predicted to be moving in. A sudden whack at the side of the house startled him until he recognized what had caused it.

"Ben?" Sierra's voice was hesitant.

"I'm awake."

"Did you hear that?"

"It's okay. It's a loose branch on one of the pines. I need to do some trimming."

He knew exactly why the noise from the loose branch had caused her concern. She was thinking about the package that had been left on his stoop.

The tree branch hit the side of the window again and he felt Sierra jump.

He hiked himself up to a sitting position. "I'll go cut it off, then you can get some sleep."

"No, you're not going out there alone at night."

"It will take five minutes—"

"Ben, please, no. Just..." She turned on her side toward him and reached across the space between them. "Just hold my hand. Once I fall asleep, I won't hear it."

Settling back on his pillow, he wrapped his fingers around hers. Desire rose up in him so quickly that he almost let go.

Her fingers slipped from his. "It was silly for me to ask you to do that. I'm fine, really."

Sierra had a bad habit of telling him she was fine when she wasn't. Had she learned to do that so her parents wouldn't worry? So they'd believe she was the independent child that they wanted her to be? Did she believe by telling herself she was fine over and over again, it would become true? Thinking about her and what she'd been through lately, he shifted on his side to face her, too, reclaimed her hand and sandwiched it between both of his.

"I guess this isn't what you expected your wedding night to be, is it?" she murmured.

"Honestly, I never expected to *have* a wedding night. I guess you're thinking about how different this is than what you really wanted with…Travis."

When she didn't respond right away, he suspected sadness was the reason.

Eventually, she admitted, "Loving Travis seems like a lifetime ago. I have our baby to think about now. That's what's most important."

Ben wanted to place his hand on her tummy, to see or feel if there was any change there yet. Still, although he was her husband, he knew he didn't have that right. They might be married, but they were strangers in some ways… in ways that mattered.

Lying here with Sierra, holding her hand, was bittersweet. But there was hope mixed in with the aftershock of getting married—hope that they could find something good together.

The tree branch whacked again, but this time, Sierra didn't react.

"Are you really going to have a security system installed tomorrow?" she asked.

"I really am." He would do anything to keep Sierra safe. Absolutely anything.

Chapter Nine

Sierra glanced around the spare room at Ben's house, feeling almost at home. After her bed rest, she'd gotten back into her normal routine at work. Since her wedding, she'd worked some evenings, but had scheduled time off to be with Ben.

The problem was with his caseload and preparations for his trial, he was never home. Since they'd married nine days ago, she'd called him twice to see if he could meet her for lunch. But he'd been too busy. At night, they slept in the same bed, but he didn't reach for her. He didn't touch her.

Night after night she lay there, asking herself the same questions. Was he still afraid she'd lose the baby? Did he regret having married her? Sometimes when they brushed by each other in the kitchen, she saw the muscle in his jaw work. She saw his eyes darken and she imagined he wanted to kiss her.

Why didn't he?

Maybe with his family flying in tonight and Thanksgiving tomorrow, the tension and uncertainty between them would lessen.

She hoped so. She had something else to discuss with him. An e-mail had come in from her parents this afternoon. They wanted her to come to Africa! Of course that wasn't in her plans. Once she told them about her marriage and the baby, they'd see why the idea was impossible. The problem was she didn't want to just send her news in an e-mail. She wanted to tell them if they called over Thanksgiving. But she was curious how Ben would deal with the situation.

When the front door opened, Sierra easily recognized her husband's baritone. She also heard other voices. She adjusted her blouse and jeans. Her waist was thickening, but only those who knew her well could tell.

She took a deep breath, not knowing what to expect from Ben's family. Slipping her parents' e-mail into a folder—she kept all of them so they didn't get deleted or lost—she closed her laptop, stacked the folder on top and took both to the master bedroom, placing them on the corner of the dresser. Kyle would be sleeping in the smaller of the two spare rooms, the one Sierra had been using for her beading supplies.

When Sierra stepped into the living room, everyone turned to look at her. She felt as if she were being examined inside out until Ben made the introductions and his brother Nathan shook her hand. He gave her a broad smile and welcomed her to the Barclay clan. Nathan's wife, Sara, unceremoniously gave her a huge hug as if they'd known each other for a long time.

Like his father, Kyle extended his hand for a shake.

Sierra solemnly took it and gave him a smile. "I made chocolate chip cookies. Someone told me you might like them."

He broke into a huge grin. "Yeah, I'm hungry."

Ben said, "I think they need something more substantial than chocolate chip cookies. They didn't have time to get anything to eat at the airport."

"I have taco meat ready and all the fixings. We just have to warm it up," Sierra told him.

He looked surprised. "You've been busy."

"I took off early from work this afternoon to get a few things ready."

"I hope you didn't go to a lot of trouble," Sara said. "We don't want to be a bother. I can help with anything you want to do for Thanksgiving."

Sierra liked Sara already. She was obviously warm and friendly and kind. "My aunt's coming over to help, too, so we'll be having a feast."

Sara motioned to the two pies on the counter. "It looks as if you've already started."

Sierra shrugged. "I didn't want to let everything go until tomorrow."

Ben was studying her in a way that made her pulse speed up and her breath hitch a little, as if he'd admired what she'd done, as if he was grateful for it.

Suddenly his cell phone beeped.

Sierra looked at him with questioning eyes, wondering if he'd be called away. He checked the ID and said, "Be right back."

She resigned herself to the fact that he might be leaving for the evening. She knew this was a way of life for him and she just had to accept that. Even though she was his wife, she had no right to make demands, not in their situation. But she worried what would happen once the baby was born. She might be a single parent even though she was married!

While Ben was on the phone, Sierra and Sara set out a light supper, and Nathan and Kyle played crazy eights in the living room. As Sierra took the taco meat from the microwave, she said, "Ben told me that Kyle has asthma. Any precautions I should know about besides not wearing perfume?"

"As long as he takes his medication, he's good. But thanks for asking. Ben told us the baby's due at the end of May. What's the date?"

"May 23. But I've been told first babies are unpredictable."

"I bet you're so excited."

"I am."

"Will you be turning the spare room into a nursery?"

"Ben and I haven't talked about that yet."

When Sara gave her a quizzical look, Sierra felt she needed to give some explanation. "We're not your usual newlyweds."

Sara studied her. "Should we have come? Is this not a good idea? We could still stay at a motel."

"No, it's great you're here. Maybe I'll actually see Ben over the holiday." As soon as she realized what she'd said, she clamped her lips shut. "I shouldn't have said that."

Sara placed her hand on Sierra's arm. "Look, if you need to talk, I'm a good listener. The Barclay brothers—" she lowered her voice "—are complex men. Ben maybe even more so than Nathan or Sam."

"Why?" Sierra whispered back.

"I think he took their mother's desertion the hardest," Sara confided in the same low voice.

Ben returned to the room then, looking…

Sierra wasn't exactly sure what way to characterize his expression—intense, worried, determined.

Addressing Sierra, he said, "I need to talk to you for a minute." He nodded toward the bedroom.

"Supper's ready." Couldn't a conference wait? she wondered.

As if he were seeing the food on the table for the first time and his family gathered in his house, he nodded. "All right, we'll talk after supper."

During the meal, Ben was quiet. He answered questions. He forced banter with Kyle. He asked Nathan and Sara about his brother Sam, his sister-in-law Corrie, the baby and their dad and the housekeeper, Val. But Sierra could tell part of his mind was somewhere else. At least he was here, though. That was something.

Kyle was working on his second chocolate chip cookie when he leaned close to Sierra and said, "I'm going to get a brother or sister."

Ben had told Sierra that Nathan and Sara had submitted paperwork to adopt. But Sierra acted surprised. "You are?"

Sara and Nathan exchanged a look, then Nathan responded, "We *hope* you're going to get a brother or sister. There are a lot of people who want to be moms and dads to babies who don't have homes."

"I know, so you're on a long list. But when I write to Santa this year, that's what I'm going to tell him I want. It worked last year when I asked for Sara to be my mom."

Kyle's parents looked stunned.

"Val helped write the letter," he said proudly. "And she mailed it for me."

Nathan laughed and ruffled his son's hair. "Well, then, maybe Santa *can* help us again this year. And if not this year, maybe next. We have to be patient."

"Uncle Sam and Aunt Corrie's baby, Diane, is my cousin," Kyle announced proudly.

"And in May you'll have another cousin," Sierra told him. "You'll have to come visit again then."

"Can we, Dad?"

"We'll have to see what happens until then."

"Is it a boy or girl?" Kyle asked.

Sierra's gaze met Ben's. He didn't look away and neither did she. "We don't know yet. We think we want to be surprised. But as soon as we know, we'll let *you* know."

A half hour later, Nathan and Sara were getting Kyle ready for bed when Ben pulled Sierra into their bedroom.

"What is it?" she asked, knowing whatever his call had been about had bothered him throughout supper.

He nodded to the chair beside the dresser. "Why don't you sit down."

But she didn't budge. "Just tell me what's wrong."

"I got a threatening call. The voice was digitally altered. Anyone can pick up one of those machines at an electronics store."

"What did he say?"

This seemed to be harder for Ben to tell her. Finally he admitted, "He knows I married you. He knows your name."

Sierra's hands protectively went to her tummy.

Ben saw and understood. "I don't think he knows about the baby. He didn't mention it. But I don't want your name on his lips."

"If the voice was digitally altered—"

"I know who it was. It was Al Levsin, the brother of a man I'm prosecuting. The trial starts soon. He's trying to shake me up before it does, but he won't. The police department brought him in for questioning, but he kept silent and wouldn't admit anything. So…I have a friend who's a former cop who's going to keep an eye on you."

"Follow me?"

"Sort of. At least until the trial's over."

"Do you have to pay for this protection?"

"He's retired and is doing it as a favor, but yes, I'll pay him."

"Is there anything I should know? Anything I should do?" The idea she was in danger was so far-fetched, so removed from normal life, it was difficult to assimilate the threat.

"Just the usual precautions. You have to use common sense. You should be safe at your shop with customers and people around. When you come home, drive directly into the carport and come inside. Dave—my friend's name is Dave Brickner—will make sure you're inside with the alarm on before he leaves."

"Do you really think this is necessary?"

"I have no idea, but I'm not taking any chances."

"Uncle Ben! Aunt Sierra!" came Kyle's voice from the hall. "I want to say good-night."

"Coming," Ben called. Stepping close to Sierra, he asked, "Are you all right?"

Actually, she wasn't. More than anything, she wanted

to be held in Ben's arms. If he'd hold her, then she *would* be all right. But she just couldn't say the words. She couldn't ask him for what should come naturally between a husband and wife. She loved this man, she really did. She longed to express that love. But as Ben's sister-in-law had said, Ben was complicated. He'd let her into a portion of his life, but he still had his guard up. He wasn't opening his heart any more than his arms. She wanted to break through his barriers and reach into the man he really was, but she didn't know how to do that.

"Let's go say good-night to Kyle," she murmured. "Maybe after Sara and Nathan go to bed, we can talk more."

She hoped they could. Maybe talking would lead to understanding. She had to know if she was more than a responsibility to him, if he really cared about her. If he didn't, then she didn't know what was going to happen to their marriage or to their future.

When Ben came to their bedroom, it was 2:00 a.m.

Sierra turned toward him in the dark. "I'm awake. Go ahead and switch on the light."

The evening hadn't gone exactly as she'd planned. The four of them had talked for a while, though Nathan and Ben had fallen into a conversation and both Sara and Sierra had seen the brothers had catching up to do. Sara had excused herself and gone to bed around midnight. So had Sierra. But she hadn't been able to sleep, thinking about Ben's phone call earlier and what he planned to do for her.

At the dresser, Ben turned on the light. He went into the bathroom and a few minutes later came out in his sleeping shorts, his jeans over his arm. "I didn't mean to stay up so late."

"You and Nathan had a lot to talk about. It's different speaking face-to-face than over the phone."

"Yeah, I guess it is."

"Is everything okay in Rapid Creek?"

"It seems to be. Dad's been having some blood pressure problems he didn't tell me about, but Nathan said the doc's controlling it with meds."

"Your father doesn't want you to worry."

"I worry more when I'm not in the loop. Nathan thinks Dad and Val are actually thinking about getting married. They're talking about eloping to Las Vegas after Christmas."

Ben sounded astounded by the idea, and she remembered what Sara said about Ben being the one who minded most when his mother left. "How would you feel about your dad getting remarried?"

Ben folded his jeans over the back of the chair slowly, as if the question made him uncomfortable, but he replied, "I'm fine with it if that's what he wants."

"But how do you *feel?*" Sierra pressed. "About Val, I mean."

"Val's great. I don't know her as well as Nathan and Sam do, but I'm sure we'd get along okay."

After a few moments of heavy silence, Sierra asked, "Did you tell Nathan what's going on concerning the trial?"

She turned on her side to face her husband, to try to figure out exactly what he was thinking and feeling.

"Yeah, I did. I wanted him to be aware of what was happening while he was here. That's only fair to him and Sara. I thought since he's so protective of Sara and Kyle, he'd want to move them to a B and B. But he seems to think there's safety in numbers. Since they'll be doing the touristy thing Friday and Saturday away from the house, he doesn't see why they shouldn't stay here."

"Do you really believe we're in danger?"

"I think Al Levsin is using scare tactics to scramble my focus on the trial. I don't think he wants to go to jail any more than his brother, and he won't do anything to put himself there. After all, he's done everything he could to make the threats anonymous except for the one, so I knew who I was dealing with. There were no prints on the box or evidence on the rat. He's playing a game and hopes it will be enough to get me to throw the trial."

Lifting his jeans from the chair, he took his wallet out of his pocket and tossed it to the wooden valet on the dresser. When he did, it hit the corner of the folder on top of the laptop and knocked it to the floor. Paper scattered everywhere.

Stooping, he gathered it all up. "What are these?"

"My parents' e-mails."

The one from today had landed on the top and his eyes scanned it.

She knew the words he was reading.

Sierra,

We know our not being able to come home for Thanksgiving was a disappointment to you. Of course we'd like to see you again. You're our daughter and every day we wonder how you are. So after your dad and I talked about it, we decided to make a suggestion to you. We know you enjoy your bead shop and living with Gina, but we also know you like to help people, too, as you did in the clinic in Africa. We know you haven't forgotten Travis and maybe you won't get over him until you do something about it. While we are continuing our research, we're also involved with a humanitarian group that is setting up a school. What we were thinking was that you could teach there. You love children. You know the dialects. You could teach English and anything else basic you feel capable of. Please think about it, Sierra. You could do a lot of good here.

Love,

Mom and Dad

As Ben finished reading the e-mail, his jaw went hard. "You haven't told your parents yet that we're married and you're pregnant?"

"I didn't want to just write it in an e-mail. I was going to ask you how you might handle it. They might call over the holiday and I can tell them then."

He glanced at the e-mail and then back at her as if he wasn't sure whether he could believe her or not. "And what about teaching at this school? Is that something you've wanted to do?"

"In the past. But now I'm pregnant and married to you."

Slowly, he closed the folder and set it on top of the laptop. Then he switched off the light.

As he slid into bed under the sheet, she moved closer to him. "Ben."

"It's late, Sierra."

"Not telling my parents doesn't mean anything. We're

not close like your family. We're thousands of miles apart, and the truth is, I'm embarrassed about how this happened."

His voice was low in the silent room, but she could hear him clearly. "I keep forgetting you're only twenty-four."

"What does *that* have to do with anything?"

"You're still young enough to want your parents' approval."

"Are you saying you don't care if your dad approves of what you do?"

"I'm saying I'm old enough to make my own decisions and cut my own path. It's nice if my dad approves, but it's not essential."

"Maybe that's because you know your dad will support what you do. I've never had that kind of support from my parents. Keep in mind, Ben, I didn't ask them if I should get married. I did it because it was the right thing for me to do."

Because she loved him.

But she couldn't tell him that—not yet. He still wasn't sure he wanted to be married to her, that was obvious. He wanted to be a dad, but did he want to be a husband? She wouldn't plead with him to make love to her. After all, she had her pride, too. It was so obvious he didn't trust what she said. He had so many walls around his heart, she didn't know if she could ever break through them.

She rested her hands on her stomach, connecting with the child there, believing this baby would lead them into the marriage they were supposed to have. She hoped so, because she wasn't sure what direction to take next. She loved Ben, but if he didn't love her, where would they go from here?

* * *

On Thanksgiving Day, Ben played games with Kyle and Nathan on the Xbox he'd rented while they were visiting. The whole time, however, he was aware of Sierra, Sara and Gina working in the kitchen, talking and laughing as if they were all old friends.

The laughing stopped whenever he went near Sierra, though, and he knew at some point they'd have to clear the air. He hated the tension between them, but it came from so many things, frustrated sexual desire at the top of the list. He didn't want to want her, but damn it, he did. Whenever he was in the same room with her, whenever he looked at her, whenever she looked at him, whenever he got too close. His mind should be analyzing, preparing and reviewing for the trial that was coming up fast, instead of thinking about this desire for Sierra.

Passing the game control to Kyle, he joked, "You beat your dad now. I've got to set up folding chairs."

"Need help?" Nathan asked.

Ben waved away his offer as he headed for the spare-room closet. He'd removed two chairs from the stack of four there and closed the closet door when his sister-in-law entered the room. As his gaze fell on her, he knew Sara had something on her mind.

"Looking for something of Kyle's?" he asked. Some of his nephew's clothes were strewn across the bed.

"No, looking for you." Sara closed the door behind her and approached him. "Remember last Thanksgiving?"

He did, indeed, remember last year. He'd met Sara for the first time at Nathan's home. "I sure do."

"You thought Nathan had made a mistake asking me to spend Thanksgiving with him and Kyle."

"Yes, I did. But by the time I caught my flight out, I wasn't so sure. I think I started to like you right away because you honestly answered every question I put to you."

"I liked you, too. I knew you were just being protective of Nathan and Kyle."

"We've come a long way," he admitted.

"I think of us as friends now," she suggested. "Sometimes you can be part of a family and not really *be* friends."

Ben propped the chairs against the closet door. "So, what's on your mind, *friend?*"

She laughed. "Nathan told me not to meddle."

"But you don't listen to Nathan when your intuition tells you otherwise." She'd been a matchmaker against his brother's advice for Val and their dad. She'd also done a little matchmaking between Corrie and Sam.

"I don't want to step where I shouldn't," she said, serious now. "But you and Sierra seem so tense around each other. Is there anything I can do to help? Maybe we shouldn't be staying here with you."

"Has Sierra said something?"

"No, she wouldn't. I mean, not intentionally."

"Not intentionally?"

"I get the idea that she thinks you work the hours you do to avoid her."

"That's crazy!"

"Is it? I mean, I know you work long hours…" She trailed off.

"I'm preparing for a trial. You know what my caseload's like. Or maybe you don't. At any one time I can be carrying eighty cases."

Sara looked shocked.

"They don't all require my immediate attention at the same time, but they're there."

"Did you and Sierra talk about this before you got married?"

"No. The baby was the reason we got married. That's no secret."

Now Sara looked troubled. "Ben, if that's the only reason—"

"It's not the only reason." He wasn't going to go into the kind of attraction he and Sierra shared, with Sara.

"When I asked Sierra about the wedding, if anyone had taken any pictures, she looked embarrassed, just said it all happened so fast, no one thought to bring a camera. She said she'd always imagined she'd get married in a church."

He knew Sierra went to mass every Sunday except for her time on bed rest. He'd pushed for them to get married quickly and she'd kept quiet about her wants. What else had she kept quiet about?

"Let me ask you something," Ben asked abruptly. "Nathan's twelve years older than you are. Has that been a problem?"

"Problem? No. It never comes up. Why?"

Ben raked his hand through his hair. "Because I'm eleven years older than Sierra and sometimes I think, sometimes I feel as if I've pushed her into marriage. If she'd had more time to think about it, maybe she would have decided not to marry me."

"Sierra seems to know what she wants. I don't get the feeling she'd let anyone else tell her what to do. But then I've only known her two days."

"She would have been married a few years ago, but

her fiancé was killed. I'm not sure she's over him or over what happened."

"Have you talked about this?"

"Some, not a lot. I know it's painful for her."

"Sometimes when two people walk through the pain together, it brings them closer." Sara looked down at her hands and then back up at him. "Do you want to get closer to her, Ben? Or are you protecting yourself in case it doesn't work out?"

That question packed a wallop. How close had he actually ever been to a woman? He remembered Lois's comment about feeling alone when she was in the same room with him. Did Sierra feel that way, too? Did she feel as if they didn't really have bonds? As if they were cohabitating simply for the sake of the baby?

That's exactly what they were doing.

Sara laid her hand on Ben's shoulder. "I want to see you happy. I want you to be as happy as Sam and Corrie and Nathan and I are."

"You're asking for a miracle."

"Don't you realize it's that time of year?" Her eyes twinkled.

"You're an eternal optimist," he accused her.

"I'll take that as a compliment."

He laughed. "I'll have to make sure Nathan buys you something special for Christmas this year. You deserve it."

"We all deserve to be happy."

Ben was reminded of Sara's comment later that afternoon after everyone had eaten the feast. There had been so much food he didn't know if there was room in the refrigerator for all the leftovers. When he carried the turkey pan to the sink, he found Sierra separating the leftovers. Her silky hair, her pretty smile, always drew him closer and today was no exception, even with the tension between them.

"Are you giving your aunt some to take home?" he asked.

"Yes, but I'm also making up packages for a family I know. I'll drop them off before work tomorrow."

"A family who didn't have Thanksgiving dinner?"

"If they had it, I'm sure it was nothing like this."

"Would you like to drop off the food this evening?"

"I didn't want to be rude and leave your family."

"They won't mind. When your aunt leaves, I can drive you."

"That would be great! Thank you for suggesting it. I didn't want to break up the party."

He absolutely couldn't stay away from her. He just couldn't. Cupping her chin in his hand, he looked deep into her eyes. "Sierra, this is your family now, *your* life, too."

She didn't look away and neither did he. The current that had been between them from the moment they met snapped and sparked. He wanted to kiss her more than he wanted to breathe. But a kiss like that would lead to the bedroom, and they simply couldn't do that right now with her aunt and his family about twenty feet away. And later?

Later, he'd probably be going over all the reasons why he should stay away from his new wife. He remembered the e-mail from her parents, the parents she hadn't informed of their marriage. He remembered her late fiancé, Travis, and how deep her memories of the man probably ran. He remembered their hurried ceremony at the justice of the peace and Sierra's desire for a church wedding. He had the feeling he'd botched everything so far. He wanted to make sure he didn't botch anything else.

When he backed away, Sierra looked disappointed. So was he. But for now, backing away was better than getting too close.

Close meant pain for both of them if this didn't work out.

Chapter Ten

Sierra climbed in the passenger side of Ben's SUV, her smile broader than he'd seen it since the night he'd met her.

"Did they like the food?" he asked.

"The kids couldn't wait to dig in. They wanted to eat the turkey cold."

"You said Penny is a single mom?"

"She was divorced recently and her husband's not paying child support. She doesn't even have her GED. She's a good worker and I'd hire her myself. But my payroll can't cover another employee."

"How did you meet her?"

"She's my aunt's cleaning person. That's what she's doing to earn money. I know she's struggling to make ends meet. I want to buy a few things for the kids for Christmas and leave them on her doorstep anonymously."

He turned the key in the ignition and started up the SUV so he wouldn't reach out and touch Sierra's smile, so he wouldn't pull her into his arms for a kiss. Physical contact with her made him feel…vulnerable. He hadn't felt vulnerable since he was a kid and didn't like it one bit.

He thought about that job in the school in Africa her mother had written about. Would that suit her? Would she rather be there than here?

As he pulled away from the curb, he reflexively checked the rearview mirror. After he made a right, he checked it again.

Sierra suddenly sat up straighter. "Do you think someone might be following us?"

"Let's just say I'm on the lookout in case they are."

When he glanced at her, he saw her expression and knew immediately she was upset about something. "I'm just covering all the bases, Sierra. I don't like surprises."

"Neither do I," she murmured. "I should have known better than to think—"

"To think what?"

"Nothing." She clamped her lips shut.

If she expected that to be the end of the conversation, it wasn't. He didn't want to go back home with this much tension between them. Even Kyle would ask what was wrong.

Ben believed the best route to get anywhere he wanted to go was the direct one. Making a sudden decision, he took a right into a strip shopping center parking lot. On the holiday, it was deserted.

"Where are we going?" Sierra asked.

He pulled the car into a slot, slipped the gear into Park and switched off the ignition. "Tell me what you're thinking."

A determined, almost defiant look came into her eyes. "Why?"

The question threw him off balance. "Because you're upset about something and I want to know what that is."

"And because you want to know, I should tell you?"

"That seems reasonable to me." He was trying to be patient.

"What's reasonable to you and what's reasonable to me are two different things." She shook her head sadly. "When you said you'd drive me this afternoon, that you'd like to go along to drop off the food, I thought you were doing it—" she hesitated then went on "—because you wanted to be with me, because you wanted to share something with me, because you just might like the idea of us being together in the midst of holiday and family and...everything." She turned away from him and looked out the window. "But that wasn't it at all. You said you'd drive because you wanted to protect me."

He could feel the hurt he never meant to cause her and he didn't like feeling guilty. Damn it, he hadn't done anything wrong! "Of course I wanted to protect you. We're married now. You've been threatened. Did you think I was going to let you just drive off alone?"

"That's not the point, Ben," she said wearily. "That's not the point at all."

When she shifted to face him once more, the sheen in her eyes made his gut clench.

He unfastened his seat belt and moved closer to her. "You're blowing this out of proportion."

"No, I don't think I am. We're married, Ben. Is it so unreasonable for me to want you to want me?"

Her words shocked him. He'd been giving her space

and time because he thought it was best. He'd been lying in that bed night after night, not wanting her to feel obliged to have to do anything she wasn't ready for. And now, as he looked at her flushed face, her bright eyes, the desire he so plainly felt, too, the restraint he'd counted on for all of his life cracked and split in two.

Unfastening her seat belt, his gaze never wavering from hers, he held her chin in his hand and took the kiss that had been days in waiting…weeks in waiting. He didn't care about finesse or expertise. At that moment, he didn't care if he even shook her up a little. She wanted to be wanted. Well, he wanted her, all right, and he was going to show her. His tongue breached her lips, searching for the pleasure they both needed.

Sierra's hands gripped his shoulders, whether from a startled response or in reaction, he couldn't tell. Controlling his sexual needs had never been a problem, but he couldn't access his control button at that moment and didn't even want to try. Sierra's soft moan, her fingers tightening and releasing, her tongue stroking against his, told him she was as into the kiss as he was. He should stop, he really should. But her hair sliding against his cheek, the velvet sweetness of her mouth, stoked his passion and sent his heart beating practically out of his chest. All he wanted to do was rip off his clothes, rip off her clothes, and have a roaring good time, right here in his SUV. But the last thing he needed was a cop cruising by, stopping to take a look. He wasn't a kid in his teens and he had more sense than that.

If he could find it.

Finally he ended the kiss and broke away.

Looking dazed, Sierra blinked. "Where did that come from?" she murmured.

"It's been brewing."

"I didn't know. All those nights in bed, I just thought you didn't care."

"You know I care about you and the baby. That's why I married you."

"You married me so you could be a dad."

He couldn't deny that, because that was the truth of it. He wouldn't take the chance on a custody agreement or a prejudiced judge or the whim of a woman who could be like his mother if given the chance. Most women were selfish. Wasn't that the subliminal message his father had always given him?

"You still don't trust me, do you, Ben?" Sierra asked, looking disappointed. "You don't trust my word or my commitment or what I want from you. *Do* you believe this baby is yours?"

Gazing into her eyes, thinking about everything that had happened, Sierra's background, along with her star-crossed first love affair, he admitted, "I believe you're telling the truth and this baby is mine."

"Thank heaven for small miracles," Sierra murmured, and turned away from him, staring out the side window.

Since there didn't seem to be any more to say, since Sierra wouldn't make eye contact and he didn't think hauling her into his arms in the middle of the parking lot would get them any further than it had already, he started up the SUV, took another long look in the rearview mirror and headed home.

Sierra turned off the water in the sunken tile tub Thanksgiving night, hoping to find peace of mind. She'd known marriage to Ben would be rocky but—

The bathroom door suddenly opened and her husband stood there naked. "Mind if I join you?"

Her mouth went dry as sawdust as she stared at Ben's body and felt the raw sex appeal that emanated from him. His chest was covered with black hair. Her gaze drifted below his navel.

"If you want a private bath, I can get a shower when you're finished," he said, his voice gravelly.

Since they'd been married, they hadn't gone to bed at the same time. They hadn't shared the bathroom. They hadn't been naked in each other's presence.

The sunken tub wasn't oversize, but it was big enough for two. If she said yes to him joining her, she might be saying yes to a lot more. She hoped she was, but she was afraid to hope for too much. "The water's just right. Come on in."

She thought she saw relief on Ben's face. Had this been a hard step for him to take?

He closed the bathroom door and turned the lock. "Privacy," he explained. "Kyle could have a bad dream and go to the wrong room by mistake, though I doubt it."

The truth was, they probably had more privacy here than anywhere in the house. The bathroom was on the outside wall of the bedroom, well insulated with its tile and adobe. The walk-in closet was on the other side of it lining the hall.

Ben came up the two steps, sat on the edge of the tub and swung his legs into it.

Sierra couldn't keep her gaze from him, couldn't help but admire the muscles in his thighs, his flat stomach, the athletic grace with which he moved. When he sank into the water and sat at one end of the tub, his legs brushed hers as he stretched them out. "Sara's as excited about coming to your shop tomorrow as Kyle is about visiting the petroglyphs."

It was obvious Ben was trying to put them both at ease, but with his body lodged against hers, that wasn't going to happen.

"I thought..." She tried again when her voice came out sounding wobbly. "I thought I'd let Sara pick out something she likes to take with her."

Ben's voice was husky when he said, "The two of you seem to be getting along well."

"She's so easy to talk to."

"That she is," Ben agreed. Then he confessed, "At first I thought it was an act so I'd approve of her in Nathan's life. But she's the real deal."

So he hadn't trusted Sara's motives, either, Sierra thought. That shouldn't surprise her. He was a strong man, filled with integrity and deep moral values. But he had so many walls around his heart she didn't know if she could ever break through them. Yet he'd come in here tonight and slipped into the tub with her. She was afraid to do or say the wrong thing, so she kept silent, glancing at him and then away.

Ben shifted his legs in the water and went still again. "Sierra."

When Sierra's gaze met his, she was shaken by the turbulence there.

"Why did you come in here tonight?" she asked softly.

"Why did you agree to let me come in?"

Would they always be at a stalemate? They would unless she let her defenses go, unless she took the first real step. "I want our marriage to work."

He leaned closer. "Maybe it's time we took it to the next level. Maybe it's time we made this a real marriage." There was desire in his eyes, so much desire that her tummy somersaulted and her world spun a bit.

"How do you want to do that?" she asked lightly, trying to build a bridge, becoming more excited each minute she was alone with Ben in the tub, each moment she thought about what might come next.

He nodded to her wet hair. "Did you already wash your hair?"

She nodded.

"What about the rest?" There was a teasing, almost seductive note in his voice she didn't think she'd ever heard before.

Time to throw caution to the wind. "I'd like help with the rest. Then I could return the favor and do the same for you."

Ben lifted a pale pink net ball and a bottle of soap from the edge of the tub. After he wet the ball, he poured a little of the liquid on it and worked it into a lather.

"This will be easier if you're within reaching distance."

Yes, so much easier, and so much more heart thumpingly intoxicating. She shifted to her knees and so did he.

They were face-to-face, naked body to naked body. They might have been sleeping together the past two weeks, but they hadn't really been naked together, not since that first night. The awareness between them was palpable.

"You're so beautiful." His voice was raspy and she could see the desire she was feeling, too. It set his jaw and tautened his body.

Her body, on the other hand, just wanted to lean into his, to feel his strength and the masculine planes she'd known once before.

Her hair was wet, and he brushed it off her shoulders until it swung down her back. Then he took the net ball and spread lather across her collarbone. The titillation excited her, but she wanted his hands on her more. Maybe he'd get the idea if she used hers. Lifting the bottle of soap, she poured some of the liquid into her hands, created a lather, then reached for his shoulders.

He braced himself, and she smiled. "Relax. This is going to feel good."

"If it feels too good, we're not going to get much past soaping." His tone was raw.

"Soaping is good," she teased as she lathered his chest hair slowly, letting her thumbs twirl in it, dragging her fingers down his chest.

He groaned. "I'm supposed to be washing *you.*"

"We can both work at the same time."

He laughed then—a genuine laugh. "I suppose we can." Tossing the ball to the corner of the tub, he splayed his hands over her breasts and her breath hitched.

"Not so simple anymore, is it?" he asked.

The question was rhetorical and she couldn't have answered if her life depended on it. Ben leaned in for a kiss while his hands moved over her body. The water seemed to intensify every sensation, the glide and slide of his fingers, the meeting of skin against skin. His kiss started slow as a teasing temptation that soon turned hungry. The demands of his tongue left her breathless as she held on to him, and reveled in each moment of closeness. She wanted this interlude to go on forever.

Ben angled the kiss to take it deeper and pressed her against him by running his hands down her back, over her buttocks until they were nestled tightly together. But it wasn't enough. She wanted him inside her. She wanted to feel him hot and hard and huge, filling her.

He must have wanted the same thing, because he broke the kiss and murmured in her ear, "Straddle me."

He leaned back with her on top of him, and her legs slid around him. He didn't hurry to join them, rather just let their bodies sink together, slipping against each other, his hands locked behind her. His mouth found the curve of her neck. The trail of kisses to her earlobe made her restless and she reached between them, sliding her hand below his navel. He groaned when she caressed him. As she felt a shudder go through his body, she felt empowered that her touch could arouse him so.

After he sucked her earlobe into his mouth one more time, he asked, "Are you ready?"

Leaning back, she stroked his jaw. "More than ready."

She was hoping he would smile at her and tease her again. Instead his mouth became a tight line and the muscle in his jaw jumped. Holding her hips, he pushed inside her. She reveled in the fulfillment and sensations that tingled through her.

He gave a deep, guttural groan as he drove completely into her, and she held on to his shoulders to ground herself. The water seemed to magnify each of his thrusts. She felt as light as a feather, yet every sensation of his body inside hers created fireworks that danced down every one of her nerve endings.

"Oh, Ben!" She was close to tears because the pleasure was so wonderful. The words "I love you" almost came tumbling out, but she held them back, fearing they'd put a stop to everything. Still, she felt them and she hoped *he* felt them as she rocked with him, gave back his hard kisses and came undone in his arms.

Ben shuddered, and then his complete stillness told her he'd found his release, too. She didn't want to separate from him ever, but he shifted and she just knew he was going to push her away.

Because?

Because they'd just been as intimate as two people could be.

He backed away. "Are you okay?"

Of course he'd ask that. He was the protector. "I'm great. How about you?"

He obviously hadn't expected that question. "I'm good."

"As good as the first time?" she teased, hoping to lighten his mood.

"Different from the first time, but just as good."

He was talking about the physical sensations and she was talking about so much more. "I guess it's hard to snuggle afterward in a tub."

"That's what you want to do? Snuggle?"

"Only…only if it's what *you* want to do." She shook her head. "Ben, this shouldn't be so hard. I mean, we just had a wonderful experience and…"

But maybe he hadn't had such a wonderful experience. She had no idea what was going on in his head because he wouldn't tell her.

He leaned toward her, kissed her on the lips and pulled away. "I'll meet you in bed to snuggle."

There was something in his voice that made her defiantly want to say, *Forget it. Don't do this out of duty. Don't do it because you want to keep me happy so I don't run away with your child.* Yet she knew better than to cut off her nose to spite her face. Maybe in duty, Ben would realize she loved him. Maybe *he'd* realize he felt more than responsibility for her.

Maybe.

As he sat on the edge of the tub and then rose to his feet, Sierra admired everything about him all over again. He was her husband…her husband.

So why didn't the word mean as much as it should?

It was sex in the bathtub.

Ben tried to put what had happened in the bathroom into perspective as he dried off and tossed his towel onto a chair. It had started out differently than it had ended. Sierra had wanted to take a step forward in their marriage, seal their union, assure them both they were husband and wife in a real way. Having sex with Sierra on the night he'd met her had been mind-boggling. They'd fallen into it… erupted into it. There was no awkwardness between them. It was as if they'd known each other's bodies and needs for a long time. After the fact, he thought he'd imagined it, the synchronicity of it, anyway. But tonight brought the first night back and how it had shaken him.

Tonight their session in the bathtub had rocked him even more. He'd felt defenseless. What if she left? Not only Albuquerque, but the country? His mother had done that. She'd fled to England to find a future that hadn't included her husband and sons. Ben felt he'd had a rock in his gut ever since Sierra had told him she was pregnant. It hadn't gone away. Maybe tonight it had for that very brief interlude…mere minutes. But now it was back, heavy and solid.

Ben climbed into bed, waiting for his wife, waiting to see what her reaction would be when she reentered the bedroom.

The bathroom door opened and she'd dried her hair and put on one of those sliplike nightgowns she always wore. It was silky and molded to her when she walked. Her breasts were getting fuller. They'd felt so right in his hands….

Sierra's phone sitting in its charger on the dresser played a lilting melody.

She didn't hesitate to say, "I'll just let it go to voice mail."

"Check and see who's calling."

When she picked up the phone and checked the screen, her face broke into a radiant smile. "It's my parents!"

"Do you want some privacy?"

"No. Stay. They might want to talk to you after I tell them our news."

Or not, he thought.

Ben hardly noticed that his hands were clenched while Sierra began her conversation with small talk, asking where her parents were and what they'd done for the holiday. Finally she plunged in. "I have some news here, too. I got married. My husband, Ben, and I are having a baby in May."

Unable to take his gaze from Sierra's face, he watched her expression as she listened to whatever her mom said. "Yes, it was fast. I met him at the end of summer."

Apparently they asked another question.

"He's from Minnesota, but he's lived in Albuquerque the past nine years. He's an assistant district attorney."

When Sierra seemed to be waiting for something, Ben arched his brows. She held her palm over the mouthpiece. "Mom wanted to talk to Dad about something."

"Our marriage?"

"I'm not sure."

Then Sierra was listening again. "Oh, that would be great! I'd love to see *you,* too. Only, I was going to go with Ben to meet his family over Christmas. Hold on a minute."

She turned to him. "My parents were discussing coming home over Christmas and now Mom's sure about it. Of course they want to meet you. What should I tell them? I mean, I could stay here and you could go have Christmas with your family."

Everything inside of Ben said that that was a very bad idea. Yet a compromise in this situation would be tough. His family wanted to meet Sierra and he wanted to spend time with them. On the other hand, meeting her parents was important, too. If they started doing things separately, they'd keep on doing things separately, and that didn't sit well with him.

"Do you know when they'll be flying in?"

Sierra asked. Eventually she came back with "They're not sure of their plans yet. They're going to e-mail me when they've firmed up everything."

"Your time is up on the phone?" Sierra asked with dismay. "Oh, I see. There are other people waiting to use it. All right. Yes, I'll tell him. I'll watch for your e-mail."

And then the conversation was over.

"Tell me what?" Ben asked.

"They want you to know they're eager to meet you."

Ben's mind was already analyzing his options. "If they're flying in before Christmas, we could spend Christmas Eve with them, fly to Minnesota on Christmas Day and spend the evening with my family. I can only take a few days off. If we fly back and your parents are still here, we'll have more time with them."

"Before they go back to Africa."

Was there a wistfulness in Sierra's tone? Ben couldn't be sure.

Sierra laid her phone on the dresser and came around the bed, pulling down the sheet on her side.

"How did they take your news?"

"Mom was shocked. She told Dad."

"What did your father say?"

"He said he hoped we were planning a wedding before I found out I was pregnant."

Sierra's father obviously wanted to believe that the baby came from their relationship and not the other way around. In person, he and Sierra would have to answer all their questions and allay their fears.

"Actually, I'm surprised Mom sounded as concerned as she did," Sierra mused.

"They're your parents."

"I know, but they have a hands-off philosophy. They've always wanted me to make my own decisions and I have. When I fell in love with Travis, they just accepted that as part of my life."

"I think when someone becomes a grandparent, it's a turning point in his or her life. Maybe a grandchild will change the way they see you."

As Sierra slid her legs under the sheet, Ben couldn't help but remember how those legs felt around him, how his hands had caressed their curves. He wanted her all over again.

"Should I turn out the light?" she asked.

Ben suddenly wished he didn't own a king-size bed. If they were in an old-fashioned double bed, they'd be close to each other again.

"Go ahead," he suggested, propping his arm under his head, warning himself Sierra would probably want to go to sleep.

The sheet and cover rustled as Sierra moved about, finally settling on a position. She was across the bed, but facing him. "Ben?"

"What?"

"Can I ask you something?"

"Ask away."

"Earlier, in the bathtub… Did I satisfy you?"

The question so completely took him off guard, he turned toward her. "*Yes,* you satisfied me. Did I satisfy you?"

"*Beyond* satisfaction. You make me come apart. Do you know what I mean?"

She was so utterly honest that he quickly did away with the distance between them and wrapped his arm around her. "I know exactly what you mean," he murmured.

Her lips were very close to his when she whispered, "When you touch me, I feel like I'm on fire."

"What about when I kiss you?"

She didn't need to answer because the moment his lips took hers, she responded to him, kissing him back with as much heat as he was kissing her. He was beginning to believe he couldn't get enough of Sierra, and that truth troubled him more than comforted him.

Chapter Eleven

"I love everything in the shop!" Sara's smile was broad. "And Christmas *is* coming," she hinted to Nathan.

The Friday after Thanksgiving was probably Sierra's busiest day of the year. She'd advised Sara to come in near closing time so she could give her sister-in-law her full attention. Ben was supposed to meet them so they could all go to dinner.

"So how were the petroglyphs?" Sierra asked Kyle.

"Super! They're older than Gramps."

Nathan laughed as Sara wandered over to another corner of the shop to peek in a case. As she did, Nathan murmured to Sierra, "Can you pick out a set she likes and wrap it for me?"

"Sure I can. Do you want a necklace, bracelet and earrings?"

He nodded.

Sara was pointing to a jewelry display. "I think I'd like this turquoise-and-jasper one for Corrie. It's something she could wear with her casual clothes."

As Sierra crossed the room to remove the necklace, the bell on the door dinged and Ben came in. He'd left before she was up this morning. Everything about last night came rushing back. In between customers, visions of the two of them in the bathtub and in their bed had flowed through her mind all day.

Ben's gaze met hers, and the impact of the collision made her tremble. The heat there told her he remembered last night as vividly as she did.

After hellos all around, he asked her, "Busy day?"

"Terrifically. But that's good. How about you?"

"Busy. I just dropped in to tell you I can't go along to supper. I have to stop at the police department. I have a meeting with a detective there."

She knew better than to ask, "This late?" She knew better than to say, "On a Friday night?" There were no time restraints on crime and criminals and the work Ben did. She was terribly disappointed he wouldn't be coming with them, but she wasn't going to let him know. Still, she asked hopefully, "Do you want us to wait for you?"

"No. I don't know how long this will go on. And Kyle will be asleep in his food if you don't take him for supper soon."

Nathan crossed to his brother's side. "You can't come along?"

"Afraid not. But I promised Kyle I'd take him to Madrid, which is an old mining village, tomorrow. Afterward we can drive up to Santa Fe and do the tourist thing. What do you think?"

Sara came to join them. "Do you have to be in the shop tomorrow?" she asked Sierra.

"I should be here for a few hours," she answered, torn between caring for her business and wanting to spend time with Ben and his family.

"I'll drive you in first thing," Ben told her. "Then we can pick you up before we drive to Santa Fe. Is that okay?"

"That should work. But Ben, do you really think you have to drive me here?"

"Yes, I really think I have to."

It was so hard to tell with Ben how much of his protective nature came from his sense of responsibility or because he really cared. She'd like to think it was a mixture, and that was okay for now.

Nathan frowned. "You believe if this Levsin brother knows we're watching over Sierra he'll stay away?"

"Yes, I think he will."

"Are you sure you can take the time off tomorrow with the trial starting Monday?" Sara, who was also a lawyer, asked him. "I remember trial preparation. I never seemed to have enough hours before it began."

"After I take you to the airport Sunday, I'll have the rest of the day to finish preparing."

"When you come home over Christmas you'll have to decide if you're going to stay with us or Corrie and Sam this time. I don't think there will be enough room for you to bunk with Dad like you usually do," Nathan said.

"I don't know what's going to happen over the holidays," Ben admitted. "We might not be there for Christmas. Sierra's parents are flying in."

Both Sara and Nathan looked disappointed, but Sara

was quick to say, "You must be thrilled to see your parents. It's been a while, hasn't it?"

"It's been a year and a half," Sierra confessed.

"Maybe instead of Christmas we'll aim for New Year's," Ben offered. "I'll make flight arrangements as soon as we hear from Sierra's parents."

There were a few moments of awkwardness, and Sierra wondered again if Ben shouldn't just go home for Christmas and she'd stay in Albuquerque. She hated the thought, but she didn't want him to miss out on holiday time with his family. They'd have to talk about it again later when they were alone.

When they were alone. Would Ben desire her again tonight? Or would he simply want to go to sleep after a long day?

He checked his watch and asked Sierra, "Are you ready to close up?"

"As soon as I pull a necklace from the case for Corrie and Sara picks one she likes for herself."

"Good. I'll walk you to your car and then Nathan can follow you to the restaurant."

Ten minutes later Sierra had set the store's alarm system and was walking beside Ben to her car. As she unlocked the driver side, he moved very close to her, his arms sliding around her waist. She turned in to him, feeling breathless and excited and ready to be close.

"It might be late when I get in. Don't feel you have to wait up," he suggested.

She could smell the lingering scent of his cologne. His hair was disheveled as if he'd run his fingers through it, and *she'd* like to do the same. There were fatigue lines around his eyes, and she longed to ease them away…to kiss them away. But Nathan, Sara and Kyle were climbing into their car and they were standing in a public parking lot.

"I'll try to wait up," she assured him. "But if I fall asleep, wake me. Okay?"

"If you fall asleep, you need to sleep," he replied gently. "You didn't spend all day today on your feet in the shop, did you?"

"No. When my part-time holiday clerk came, I spent a couple of hours making jewelry this afternoon in the back room. I'm taking care of myself, Ben, and I want you to do the same. Will you get supper?"

He smiled. "Maybe I'll find a doughnut at the police department."

"Ben."

He laughed. "I'll go through the drive-through at McDonald's on the way over. Will that make you happy?"

"I don't know about happy. I'll bring something home from the restaurant and have it in the fridge. You can warm it up when you get home." She liked the idea of looking after him. Did he feel that way about looking after her?

Leaning into her, he kissed her lips soundly, but quickly. They both heard the rumble of Nathan's car and knew he was ready to follow her to the restaurant. Ben stepped away from her and she felt the loss of his presence immediately and deeply.

After she climbed into her car, he shut the door. As she watched him walk away, she knew she was falling deeper in love every day. She just wished she knew what *he* was feeling. Maybe someday soon he'd tell her.

* * *

Ben stood on his side-door stoop in the carport, listening. It was almost midnight and all was quiet. The smell of piñon pine burning in woodstoves scented the neighborhood while the dry cold seeped into him, settled, then stayed. Once again he listened in case a car had followed him up the street, in case someone had followed him, parked half a block down and was walking toward him now. The wind blew through the junipers as he unlocked the door, stepped inside and disengaged the alarm.

At first the alarm system had seemed strange and wasn't something he had thought he'd ever use. But now, as he closed the door and reset the system, he realized extra security was just part of reality.

The house was as dark and silent as the night outside. He knew his house, though, even without daylight. After he went into the kitchen and opened the refrigerator, he realized he was just too exhausted to eat. All he wanted to do was fall into bed and sink into sleep.

Making his way to the bedroom, he opened the door and stepped inside.

"Ben?"

The sound of his name on Sierra's lips sent a surge of adrenaline through him, but he told himself not to pay any attention to it. She and the baby needed a good night's sleep as much as he did. They'd have a full day again tomorrow with his family.

"Go back to sleep," he soothed. "I'll be there in a minute."

It took little more than that to visit the bathroom, discard his clothes and slide between the sheets.

Sierra inched over to him, but still didn't touch him, as if she wasn't sure how she'd be received. If only she knew.

If only she knew how much her touch and her smell and her smile affected him. If only she knew how much he fought those reactions…because if he gave into them he'd give into some kind of power she'd have over him.

"I brought home quesadillas and Christmas chili," she said.

"Too tired to eat," he mumbled.

Her foot lodged against his calf. "You're cold."

"It's cold outside."

Her foot tantalizingly slid down his calf to his instep. "Your feet are even colder. You're not going to be able to fall asleep if you're this cold."

"Wanna bet?" he joked.

Suddenly she sat up and moved to the foot of the bed.

"What are you doing?"

"I'm going to warm up your feet."

Before he had a chance to protest, her very warm hands had encircled his feet and were sharing their warmth. It felt so good to have her just sit there warming him. But then she was massaging his foot and other feelings besides warmth crept up his legs.

"Sierra—"

"Let me do this," she said softly. "You've taken such good care of me."

He hadn't done any such thing. He'd just done his duty, tried to keep her and the baby safe.

Her fingers felt wonderful everywhere they touched. And the pressure of her palms had his blood flowing faster, and not just in his feet.

Her hands were working up his legs now, and when they reached his thighs, he did protest. "Sierra, it's late."

He couldn't control his arousal. Any minute she'd know

how much he wanted her, in spite of his fatigue, and the late hour and a busy day tomorrow.

Her long hair drifted over his stomach, down to his navel, teasing him.

"Do you know what you're doing?" he asked thickly.

"The question is—do you want me to be doing it?" she returned.

"I don't want you to feel as if you owe me anything," he replied honestly.

"Owe you for taking good care of me? This has nothing to do with that. This has to do with being your wife."

He didn't know what to say to that, and as her hand enclosed him, as her head bent to him, he didn't say a word. He didn't even breathe. When she slowly rubbed her cheek against him, his hands clenched the sheets. When her tongue tasted him, his body became so taut he didn't know if it would ever relax again. Her mouth was hot, and wet and soft. It was home.

The idea captured in that one single word almost filled him with panic. A woman signifying home. A woman signifying more than pleasure. The walls he'd surrounded himself with for years seemed to slip a little on their foundation and he found himself wanting to shore them back up. But Sierra's lips, her soft, caressing touches left him defenseless.

He couldn't handle being defenseless.

"Stop." His voice was so gravelly he almost didn't recognize it.

When she looked up at him, he reached out and clasped her waist with his hands.

"Do you want me to stop altogether?" She sounded disappointed…hurt.

"Jeez, no. Sit on me." He still wanted to make sure they didn't hurt the baby. He wanted to make sure he wasn't too rough. He wanted to make sure she found pleasure, too.

Sierra pulled her nightgown up and over her head. As she revealed her body, Ben couldn't help but run his hands over her shoulders…over her breasts. When he cupped her she moaned and he again felt the new heaviness there. Her body was preparing for his baby.

His baby.

He stroked her skin, finally taking hold of her hips. When she slid onto him, he thought he'd die of the pleasure of it right there. He guided her until he was deep inside her. There wasn't a part of him that was cold now. He was on fire. And so was she. He felt her squeezing tighter around him…felt her body readying itself for release. When he touched her at exactly the right spot, she cried his name. There was so little light in the room, but he thought he caught a glimmer of a tear on her cheek. His own release rocked him, and shook him to his very core.

Moments later, as Sierra nestled into his side and he wrapped his arms around her, he wondered what had happened to the world as he'd known it. Suddenly Sierra was such a big part of it.

However, one question still plagued him. What if she left?

"This is Lois Driscoll. Is Ben Barclay home?" the unfamiliar woman's voice asked Sierra on Sunday evening.

Sierra had wandered into the kitchen to prepare supper. Ben had been working at the table in the dining area all day and she hadn't disturbed him. He was intensely preoccupied with the trial. His family had left this morning and she was going to miss them, but now that she and Ben were alone in the house, they wouldn't have to worry about being quiet in the bedroom.

As Sierra turned to Ben to tell him who was calling, the name suddenly hit her. Lois. His former girlfriend? Fear began drumming an unwelcome rhythm in her chest as she covered the mouthpiece. Maybe it *wasn't* his former girlfriend. Maybe it was another Lois.

"Ben, do you want to take this? It's a Lois Driscoll."

Ben had been studying notes on the computer, but now the name brought his gaze to hers. His expression went blank. "I'll take it," he said, pushing away from the table.

Sierra handed him the cordless receiver. "If you want privacy, I can go to the bedroom."

He glanced at the counter with its salad fixings and the pot of water on the stove heating for pasta. "No reason for you to leave," he assured her as he put the receiver to his ear.

But Sierra had a sinking feeling in her stomach that told her this was going to be a private conversation whether she stayed in the room or not. Still, there was no doubt she was going to listen to his every word.

"Hello, Lois."

Sierra took out a cutting board and began chopping a pepper.

"Yes, it *has* been a while."

Sierra minced the pepper into minute pieces.

"No, I didn't know your firm would be involved," Ben responded to something Lois said.

Sierra searched her mind for his former girlfriend's occupation. Public relations, wasn't it?

"You saw my name on the list? I see. I haven't made a decision. In fact, I've hardly had time to consider it."

When Sierra took another peek over her shoulder at Ben's face, she realized he still wasn't letting anything show.

He listened, then responded, "Yes, that's right. I got married last month. Thank you. I appreciate your good wishes."

Polite. Oh, so polite. And removed. *Was* he removed? Was his heart beating faster as he talked to Lois? Did he remember their time together? Did he wish things had worked out differently?

"Working with your firm wouldn't be awkward. We've both moved on. But thanks for calling. I appreciate your thoughtfulness."

Had a bit of warmth entered Ben's voice? Did he want to see Lois again? Would they be working together? On what?

After he crossed to the telephone base and replaced the handset, he leaned against the counter and crossed his arms over his chest. If that wasn't defensive, Sierra didn't know what was.

He studied her until she finally asked, "That was your old girlfriend?"

"I thought you'd recognize the name. Yes, it was. We haven't seen each other for a year and a half, if you wondered. We had run into each other at a fund-raiser and it was...awkward."

"So why is she calling now?"

He contemplated his answer for a few moments then launched into an explanation. "At the end of last month, someone I know approached me about leaving the D.A.'s office and taking a new position."

At the end of last month. Around the time she was worrying about losing the baby. "What kind of position?"

His arms were still crossed, but his gaze was direct. "A benefactor left an endowment to start a legal firm dedicated to helping first-time offenders. I was offered the job of setting it up and heading the team."

Although Sierra had felt she was getting to know Ben, now she realized he still hadn't let her into important parts of his life. "Are you considering the position?"

"As I told Lois, I haven't had much time to think about it."

"What does she have to do with it?"

"Apparently her firm put in a bid to do the PR work and they won the contract."

"How did she find out you were being considered?"

"Word gets around. She didn't want me to take the position and then find out about her working on it after the fact."

As Ben had said, Lois's motives could be thoughtful ones. But Sierra could also guess that the woman just wanted contact again…that maybe she was sorry they'd broken up…that maybe she'd realized what a good man Ben was. Maybe this was her way of holding out an olive branch, then pulling him toward her.

All that aside, Sierra had one other burning question. "Why didn't you mention this to me?"

"I didn't know if I wanted to consider it."

"Are you considering it?"

He pushed away from the counter and said, somewhat frustrated, "I'm not sure. There's been a lot going on."

"We're married, Ben. Decisions you make affect me. Decisions I make affect you."

"I didn't make a decision," he responded with a bit of anger now.

She knew he was under a lot of pressure with the trial starting tomorrow. She knew the work he was doing mattered. "In some ways, I don't feel as if I'm part of your life. I feel as if you shut me out."

He didn't deny it.

"*If* you take this new position—"

He started to protest.

"Just let me finish. *If* you take this new position, and *if* you're working with Lois again, will I have anything to worry about?"

She was hoping for a flicker of emotion in his eyes, on his face, something that would tell her or at least hint at what he was feeling.

But she could read nothing when he replied, "Lois and I are over. *If* I ever work with her, that relationship will have nothing to do with you and me."

Sierra wished she could believe that. But she also knew that a gap in a marriage could leave room for an interloper, or problems or disintegration altogether.

"I've got to get back to work." For Ben the discussion was closed.

His back straight, his shoulders stiff, he took a seat at the table again, rifled through a file and pulled out a typed report. Sierra felt shut out and had no idea what to do about it. If she couldn't break down Ben's barriers, then their marriage wouldn't have a chance.

On Tuesday evening, the second day of the trial, Sierra was driving to Camille and Miguel's town house. Ben wasn't home. He had a strategy meeting. He hadn't gotten home last night until after ten. It didn't take a clairvoyant to foresee this was the way it was going to be until the end of the trial.

Ever since the phone call from Lois Driscoll on Sunday, there had been a strain between them. They hadn't made love the past two nights and Sierra missed Ben in an elemental way. She would only spend a short time with her friends. She wanted to be home tonight when Ben arrived. Somehow, she'd get him to relax. Somehow she'd find a way to draw them closer together instead of wedging more of that gray space between them.

The white SUV that had been shadowing Sierra ever since she went to work yesterday morning—it was Ben's retired friend—followed her at a discreet distance. She had Dave's cell number and had informed him that she would be heading to a friend's after work rather than home. He'd assured her that was no problem.

She flipped on her turn signal a little sooner than usual to warn him she was going to take the Bernalillo exit. As she veered toward the ramp and checked her rearview mirror, she noticed a black pickup truck had cut between her and Dave. Turning off the main road, Sierra spotted headlights glaring into her rearview mirror. They were lower than Dave's. They must still be from the black pickup.

Sierra's cell phone rang. It was buried in her purse on the seat next to her, and she knew she should let the call go to voice mail. But what if it was Ben?

Plucking out the phone with one hand, she opened it and put it to her ear.

"Sierra, get off the road. Pull over *now!*"

Although she'd only spoken to him once, she recognized Dave's voice. But before she had the chance to ask a question or even find out what he meant, her car was rear-ended. She flew forward, her elbow hitting the door, then flopped back again to her seat, held secure by the seat belt. Her phone landed on the floor. What was happening?

She'd no sooner caught her breath when she was rammed again—harder this time. Dave's voice commanding that she get off the road echoed in her ears as she sped up, hoping to outrun the pickup behind her. But even through her closed windows, even through her frightened panic, she heard the roar of its engine as it pursued her once more. This time it didn't rear-end her. The pickup zoomed up beside her and crashed into her left fender.

Her wheels squealed and rubber burned as she tried to keep control. But it was no use. Her speed and the thrust of the other car against hers sent her off the side of the road into scrub pine and sage. She circled her belly with her arms as if she could protect her baby, not knowing if the car would continue to crash into her, not knowing if she would ever hear her baby's first cry.

She waited, preparing for the worst, hoping for the best, calling for Ben before she even realized his name had escaped her lips.

Chapter Twelve

"I want to talk to Sierra *now!*" Ben shouted into his cell phone.

"Calm down," Dave demanded roughly. "The paramedics are checking her out. She said she was fine, but I called them, anyway. I didn't want to take any chances with her being pregnant and all."

With her being pregnant and all.

Ben wondered if this was what it was like forever when you were a parent. Were you always afraid you'd lose your child?

"I don't think he meant to hurt her," Dave went on. "He could have done a lot more damage."

"How the hell did this happen?" Ben asked. He wanted to blame Dave. Yet deep down, he knew this was *his* fault.

"He slipped between us when we were getting off the exit."

"You saw him?"

"Are you kidding? It was dark. And before you ask, the license plate was all muddied up. I couldn't read it. That's what tipped me off. I phoned Sierra, but she didn't get off the road quick enough."

No, of course she didn't. She probably asked Dave all kinds of questions. She wasn't used to situations like this, and people who might want to hurt her. He swore so loud, Dave probably had to take the phone away from his ear.

"I see the lights," Ben muttered. "I'll be there in two minutes."

As he drove up to the scene, Ben's heart hammered hard against his chest. He screeched to a halt behind a police vehicle and headed for the paramedics van, taking his ID from his pocket in case he needed to show it. Once he spotted Sierra, some of his panic subsided. She was sitting on a blanket on the ground not far from her car, another blanket wrapped around her. She was holding a bottle of water and looked relatively okay. The fender was dented, but other than that…

His gaze targeted her again as he went to her and crouched down beside her. He wanted to take her into his arms. He wanted to touch her all over and make sure she *was* okay. He wanted to wrap her in a protective bubble until his trial was over and the danger had passed. Would the danger ever pass?

"How are you feeling?"

Her eyes locked to his, and he could tell she was holding emotion back, trying to stay calm for his sake. She didn't say she was fine. He was glad that much honesty had taken root between them.

"I called Dr. Connor," she explained, then hurriedly added, "I'm not having cramping or anything, but she said she'd meet me at the E.R., just to make sure everything is okay. But I don't want to go in the ambulance. Can you just take me?"

Ben forced his own fears back and made his voice as gentle as he could. "Of course I'll take you."

One of the police officers came up to them. "Brickner told me what happened, but I have to get a report from her."

Ben only had a passing acquaintance with the young officer, but he asked, "Can you do it at the emergency room? I'd like to get her there first and make sure everything's all right. She's pregnant."

The officer looked from Sierra to Ben. "Sure. I can do that. I'll follow you there."

Ben put his arm around Sierra and leaned close. "I'm so sorry this happened to you. It's my fault."

"No, it's *not* your fault. It's the fault of whoever did it."

He couldn't believe she wasn't blaming him because his guilt was monumental. She still might, after the shock of what had happened wore off. "I'll have to figure out a plan to keep you safe. But first, let's get you to the E.R."

Sierra clasped his arm. "The officer said they'll be taking my car. Something about testing the paint residue."

"It's evidence."

"But I need my car."

She wasn't going anywhere in her car—alone—until his trial was over. But she was already upset enough and they could talk about that after the doctor examined her. "If you need a car, we'll rent one until you get yours back. Don't worry, Sierra, I'll take care of it."

He was going to take care of everything. One way or another, he would make sure she was out of this mess. He just had to figure out how to accomplish that feat.

It was well after 10:00 p.m. when Ben drove Sierra back to his house. After several phone calls, he'd established a plan of action and was ready to present it to her. He had a feeling she wasn't going to like it. He couldn't help that. She'd never go along with what he really wanted to do, but he was going to present that to her, too. Once inside the house, she went into the living room and sank down onto the sofa. He was too wired to sit, probably because of the two cups of coffee he'd drunk at the hospital. He still had a few hours of work ahead of him, but he had to take care of Sierra first.

He shrugged out of his suit jacket and tugged off his tie, then tossed them over one of the easy chairs.

Sierra took off her jacket, laid it on the sofa next to her and rested her head against the back cushion with her eyes closed. "I'm so grateful the baby's okay."

"And that's the way we want to keep it," Ben assured her.

Catching the determination in his voice, Sierra opened her eyes and sat up straight. "Stop pacing, Ben, and tell me what's on your mind."

He hadn't even been aware he *was* pacing. Now he made himself stand still and gave her all of his attention. "You have two options."

Her eyebrows arched, and he knew that probably wasn't the best way to start, but he was beyond tact at this point.

"Those are..." she prompted, obviously holding her questions in check until she heard what he had to say.

"The first one is simple. I'll put you on a plane to Rapid Creek and you can stay with my family, out of danger, out of the state, away from me and anything that could happen because we're married."

At first she looked totally astonished. Then she just looked defiant. "I am *not* leaving. I have no intention of running away. I have a business here...a life here." She stopped abruptly. "Unless you *want* me in another state away from you. I mean, for other than the obvious reasons."

She sounded hurt, and the last thing he wanted was to hurt her or make her feel worse than she already did after what had happened tonight.

Rounding the coffee table, he sat beside her on the sofa, took her hand and looked straight into her eyes. "We have to keep you and our baby from harm."

Her eyes grew shiny, but then she cleared her throat and asked, "You said there were two options?"

"The second one's a little more complicated. Let me ask you this first. Would you consider not going into work until the trial is over?"

"No. I am *not* going to hide away somewhere and stop my life."

Most women in this position would be cowering, would be glad to be sent away someplace safe where a family could give love and protection. Most women wouldn't think twice about holing up in a safe cocoon with a guard at the door. But no, not Sierra.

"All right. If you insist on going to your shop, then

here's what's going to go down. You're going to stay with your aunt Gina. I've already spoken with her. She has an alarm system on her house already. Dave and another friend of mine are going to take shifts with you. You will not be driving. Dave will pick you up in the morning and bring you home in the evening. For the duration of this trial, you have to promise me you'll let him drive you wherever you need to go."

"Why can't I just stay here with you? Your house has an alarm now."

"Yes, it does. But I can't be here as much as you would need me to be here while this trial is going on. I want someone with you, and Gina assures me she'll stick with you like glue."

Sierra sighed. "So we'll both be prisoners."

"Only for the duration of the trial."

"What about *you?* What about *your* safety?"

"The police department is putting a man on me until the trial's over. I really don't think Levsin will hurt me. He wants to scare me."

"What happens *after* the verdict's in?" she asked, still sounding worried.

"After the verdict, there's nothing anyone can do. Not even Al Levsin. Not guilty, he won't have any reason to come after us. Guilty, there would be no point once it's over." He wasn't going to mention the possibility that Levsin might want revenge. That idea would freak out Sierra. Ben knew the police department couldn't afford to have an officer protect him forever. They were going to have to deal with this situation one day at a time.

Sierra still looked incredibly unhappy and he felt the discontent, too. Although there had been a strain since

Lois's phone call, they *were* physically closer. Their marriage had taken on a new meaning.

Encircling Sierra with his arm, he brought her to him and kissed her. It was a kiss filled with yearning and hunger and hope for better days ahead.

When he finally broke away, she asked him, "Can we go to bed now?"

He knew what she wanted. He knew what *he* wanted. But neither of them were going to be satisfied tonight. "You're going to gather your things and you're going to your aunt's."

"Now?"

"Yes, now. I have to leave early in the morning and I want you with her and safe, with Dave sitting outside the door."

She looked so vulnerable, so lovely, so worried. And he was going to miss her. He kissed her again, letting desire help them escape for just a few minutes, then pulled back, readying himself for their separation.

Separation.

He didn't like the sound of the word. He hoped this time apart wouldn't destabilize their already shaky marriage. He hoped they could hold on…for their baby's sake.

Ben walked into Gina Ruiz's house Sunday afternoon after a week-long separation from Sierra, laid eyes on his wife and felt a mixture of guilt, responsibility and longing that had gnawed at him since he'd brought her here. The trial was going well…his marriage wasn't. How could two people really be married and not live together?

Gina had opened the door to him, and the recriminations in her eyes seemed to ask the same question.

Sierra, on the other hand, smiled widely and looked as

if she'd like to run into his arms. How he wanted her there. How he'd missed her in his bed.

To her he said, "I'm sorry about last night." They'd talked on the phone every evening over the past week. Yesterday, he'd prepared witnesses for Monday, fully planning to spend the night with his wife. But he'd been called to a crime scene and had had to cancel.

As Sierra approached him, his body went tight with wanting her.

"You're here now." Her expression seemed to promise him everything they'd missed last night and more. But her aunt was here, too.

"You're taking Sierra to dinner?" Gina asked.

"Yes. Then we're going to visit Camille and Miguel." If it were up to Ben, he'd make sure they weren't tailed and then take her to a motel. But Sierra needed normalcy after what had happened to her, and their friends could provide that.

Gina's perceptive gaze targeted Sierra, and then him. She went to the foyer closet and removed her coat. "I'll be Christmas shopping and having dinner with a friend. What time will you bring Sierra home?"

"By nine."

Gina's eyebrows rose.

"I'm meeting with a detective at nine-thirty."

Gina didn't comment, but Ben felt her censure. He was putting work before an evening with his wife. He couldn't tell if Sierra was upset with their "date" being cut short or not.

After Gina gave Sierra a long hug, she nodded to Ben. "I'll make sure I'm home by nine."

For as long as Ben could remember, he hadn't cared about what other people thought concerning what he did or didn't do, as long as his conscience guided him. But Gina Ruiz's lack of enthusiasm for his marriage to Sierra bothered him. Would Sierra's parents feel the same way?

The front door closed and latched.

"You look beautiful," Ben said, meaning it. Sierra was wearing a red skirt and jacket with fringes on the cuffs. With her dark brown hair and sparkling eyes she could outshine Miss Universe, as far as he was concerned.

Her cheeks flushed. "You look spiffy, too."

Gina's car backed out of the driveway.

He crooked a finger at Sierra. "Come here. You're too far away."

As she stood before him, she asked teasingly, "Too far away for what?"

His arms encircled her. "Do you have to ask?" He sealed his lips to hers as his hands laced through her hair.

The vehemence of the kiss startled him. Sure, he'd dreamed of her every night, relived their encounter in the tub, their couplings in his bed. But he hadn't realized the extent of his need or the caliber of her response.

A date for dinner and an evening with friends had seemed to be the right thing to do. But now he understood the only alone time they'd have would be here and now, and Sierra's intentions seemed to be the same as his as she separated the lapels of his suit jacket and tried to push it from his shoulders.

"I missed you," she murmured when he broke the seal of their lips, so he could see the tiny buttons on her jacket that *he* was bent on unfastening.

There was a hint of shyness in her voice.

They were married. She shouldn't feel shy. But that small bit of reserve in her escalated his desire for her. He'd show her how much he wanted her. He'd show her she could let her passion run free with him.

Unfastening buttons and buckles was accompanied by frustrated groans when leather defied their fevered impatience, when wood buttons stubbornly stuck. Finally she freed him of his jacket, shirt, tie, shoes and slacks. As he pulled off his socks, she loosened her arms from her sleeves and the jacket fell to the floor. Her skirt and slip were easily removed as he pushed them down her hips and she shimmied free.

Catching her to him, feeling steam practically fly off of them with their bodies pressed together, he asked, "Living-room floor, sofa or bedroom?"

"I don't care," she responded breathlessly.

When he studied her face, he could see she didn't! He ground his hips against hers. "I don't think we'll make it to the bedroom."

As she passed her hands down his arms and around to his butt, he *knew* they wouldn't.

Sierra pulled down his briefs. He slid down her silky panties. He broke her landing as they collapsed to the carpet. But after their next kiss, he rolled her beneath him. He yearned to have as much of her soft skin touch his as was humanly possible. Levering himself back and forth over her, he created friction and increased their pleasure.

"You're teasing me," she breathed in short gasps.

"No, I'm getting you ready." His throat was thick with need and he could hardly push out the words.

While she nipped his neck, she slipped one small hand between them and cupped him. He couldn't even force out her name in protest. Instead, he gave in and pushed inside her.

Each time he took Sierra, he thought he'd be in control. He thought he'd know what would happen next. He thought he'd have a physical need fulfilled and he'd be satisfied once and for all.

About this, he was always wrong.

As he thrust into Sierra, she raised her knees so he could push deeper. Her satisfied sounds of pleasure goaded him on. He almost felt as if he were someone else—a caveman claiming his mate…a conqueror claiming his reward…a new man needing a woman as he never had before.

Needing Sierra.

Did she need him, too?

Or was she going along, playing along, trying as hard as she could to please him…for the sake of their baby?

When he opened his eyes, he saw hers were closed. Her hair was damp along her rosy cheeks. She'd caught her lower lip between her teeth. Suddenly he wanted to make her cry out with the greatest pleasure she'd ever known.

With a sheer act of will, he slowed his thrusts until he was staring down at her, motionless.

Opening her eyes, she asked, "Is something wrong?"

He wasn't sure. He just knew something wasn't entirely *right.*

One question blazed in his mind and shouted to make itself heard: *Will you stay?*

But he simply couldn't ask it. Because even if Sierra's answer was the one he wanted to hear, he knew at some point she could change her mind.

If she thought leaving was best for their child, he was sure she'd go.

In answer to her question, he replied, "I want this to be the best orgasm you've ever had."

She smiled, clutched his shoulders tighter and suggested, "Then don't stop."

"This isn't about racing to the finish."

"What's it about?" she asked softly with a glimmer of emotion in her eyes he couldn't decipher.

"It's about prolonging this alone time together and making the most of it."

"Do you want to start all over?" she joked.

"No." He dragged his fingers through her hair, brushing it back from her face. "I want to make it last."

He began thrusting again, slower now. In her ear he murmured, "If we were in our bathtub I'd be kissing your nipples."

He felt her tremble.

With his next prolonged entry he whispered, "All week I thought about taking your clothes off, slowly, kissing each patch of skin as I did."

"Ben—"

"What?"

"You're making me crazy."

"Good. That's just what I intended."

This time when he joined his body to hers he slid his tongue across her lips. Between kisses he said hoarsely, "The next time we're together, I'm going to lick whipped cream off a place I've never kissed before."

He felt Sierra's body begin to quiver. The ripple of pleasure spread over her and encompassed him. The reins he'd held on his control loosened as his body tensed as he pushed into her one last time. And then he was falling over the edge with her into the sublime, erotic earthquake he'd only ever known with her. With Sierra.

With his wife.

Sierra hated saying goodbye. Each goodbye with Ben filled her with fear. He was afraid for *her,* but she was afraid for *him.* Not only of the threat against him—but of him turning away…finding an excuse not to love her…an excuse to fight for his child, but not their marriage.

They stood inside the protective adobe wall at her aunt's house, both reluctant to say good-night.

Prolonging the moment, Sierra said, "Camille bought Miguel monogrammed car mats for Christmas. What's on your list?" She'd wanted to give Ben something really special, but she didn't know what that might be.

"I don't have a list. In the past, Sam, Nathan and I would find something Dad needed and, of course, presents for Kyle. But we stick to books or sports gear for one another. That might change now, though, with Sam and Nathan married. Maybe you can help with presents for Corrie and Sara—clothes or something women use."

"Do you want to go Christmas shopping together?" Nothing would please her more—except maybe for living with Ben again.

"The first break I have, we'll go. Maybe next weekend."

The starry night and the winter cold surrounded them. Ben stepped closer. "I had a great time tonight."

"Me, too." She glanced at the curb where Dave's SUV now sat. "Are you sure I can't come home with you? Dave could still drive me back and forth."

Ben's arms encircled her. "I don't want you to be alone.

This is better for you, for my peace of mind, as well as my concentration. I'll worry less this way."

She understood needing peace of mind. She spotted the unmarked car with an officer who was keeping watch over *him* and was grateful for that.

Tipping Sierra's chin up, Ben kissed her. His kiss was everything she'd always wanted a man's kiss to be. There was no doubt he desired her, that he needed her to fill a basic male hunger. But would he ever really love her? Could he love *her* as she loved him? Completely, with heart, body and soul. Being apart only intensified her worries.

He leaned his forehead against hers. "I've got to go."

"Your meeting," she reminded herself, not attempting to convey anything with her tone of voice. She knew Ben handled a multitude of cases that constantly demanded his attention. When this trial was over, there would be another one, and another after that. There would always be long hours. She could accept his job and his position. What she couldn't accept was not knowing where she stood.

That conversation was one they should have after she went home. After they were together…after they could spend day after day building a real life.

Chapter Thirteen

Ben's Monday hadn't gone as he'd planned. He'd just gotten home and hated calling Sierra this late. It was almost 11:00 p.m. When he thought about how they'd made love in her aunt's living room last night, he knew he had to hear her voice no matter how late the hour.

"How did it go today?" Sierra asked.

He was on alert immediately. Something about her tone seemed…different. "Not as well as I would have liked. The defense attorney raked one of my witnesses over the coals. When I recalled him, I tried to mitigate the damage, but I don't know if I succeeded."

"You got tied up at work because of that?"

Had she been waiting for him to call because she had something important to talk to him about? "That, and other issues I had to take care of because of not being in the office all day. How about you? What time did you get home?"

She hesitated. "One of my clerks caught the flu bug that's been going around so I stayed until closing."

He didn't like the idea of Sierra being on her feet all day at her shop. But before he could say anything about that, she revealed, "I got an e-mail from my parents today."

Ben's body tensed and he wasn't even sure why. A premonition, maybe? That note in her voice that was different?

"They're still coming before Christmas?"

"Oh, yes. They're planning to stay with Aunt Gina until mid-January." She went quiet.

"That's why they e-mailed? To tell you that?" He paced his kitchen, rubbing the back of his neck. He needed a long, hot shower and a good night's sleep. But this conversation was too important to hurry.

"That and...they made an appointment with a Professor Oppenheimer at the University of New Mexico. He's one of the main advocates for the school that's going to be established near where they're working."

"They're going to be involved in the school?" Ben asked.

"Possibly. But they really made the appointment so I could go with them to meet him."

Ben stopped. "You told them there was no point to you meeting this guy, didn't you?"

"I haven't e-mailed them back yet."

"Why not?"

"Because they went to all this trouble and I thought I might go along just as a courtesy to them."

"As a courtesy? If you go along, they'll think you're interested."

"Ben, my relationship with my parents is complicated. With all this distance between us, whenever we *are* together, I try to connect with them however I can."

He reminded himself Sierra was only twenty-four. Her childhood had been anything but normal. She wanted the closeness with her mom and dad that all children craved. He knew on some level she also needed their approval. But was she also doing this for another reason?

Their marriage wasn't a usual one, either. In fact, he wasn't even sure what the basis of it was besides the baby and their attraction to each other. Especially since they'd hardly even been together since they were married. Was she considering keeping this appointment as a fallback position? Would her parents convince her that getting married had been a mistake? Was Sierra already regretting their marriage? Regretting the baby she carried? The change of course her life would take because of it?

Now the day's fatigue really set in. "You have to do whatever you have to do, Sierra."

"Ben—"

She wanted him to understand. While part of him did, the other part didn't. "If you want to go to the appointment with them, go. But understand that what they think is best for you and what you think is best for you might be two different things. How much are you willing to give up to please them? How much are you willing to give up to stay connected to them?"

He heard Sierra's sharp intake of breath and understood that she never realized she might have to make that decision. Again, the naiveté of twenty-four versus the cynicism of thirty-five hit him hard.

"You sound angry," she said softly. "Why?"

Why, indeed? Because he was committed to the vows he'd made and she might not be? "I'm tired, Sierra, and I have to wonder why this is a decision that's difficult for you to make." He didn't want to make accusations over the phone he might regret later. He didn't want to get into an argument they couldn't untangle without them being face-to-face.

"Just because I go to this appointment and find out what they're going to be involved in doesn't mean it will affect me…or us."

"I don't believe that."

She was silent and he knew what she was thinking—he didn't trust her. Maybe that was the bottom line…he didn't.

Ben didn't call Sierra on Tuesday night and she didn't call him. On Wednesday he had a summation to prepare. On Thursday afternoon, when the trial had ended and the jury was deliberating, Ben returned to his office and checked his voice mail. There was a message from Camille. He dialed her number, though he wasn't too concerned, because Dave would have notified him if anything had happened to Sierra.

"What's up?" he asked after Camille answered.

After a moment's hesitation, she plowed in. "Miguel says I should stay out of this, that it's none of my business. But I think he's wrong. Sierra's my friend and I'm worried about her."

"Why? Has something happened?"

"I stopped in at the shop this afternoon. She said she hasn't talked to you for a couple of days."

"We've both been busy," he replied tersely, not wanting to feel guilty, but feeling it anyway.

"Do you know *how* busy?"

"I don't know what you mean."

"Sierra usually has everything under control. But two of her clerks caught the flu. She's been in her shop from eight in the morning until nine at night the past two days, with just a little help from someone she knows who cleans houses. She's planning on doing it again today."

A mixture of emotions battled for dominance. Mostly he was just angry at Sierra for not taking care of herself and the baby.

"She says she's taking breaks," Camille went on, "but she didn't seem to be herself today."

"In what way?"

"She looked really tired."

Maybe Sierra hadn't been sleeping any better than he had. "I'll stop in tonight after work and see how she's feeling."

Camille let silence stretch between them for a couple of moments. "I know your trial is hard on you, but I think it's been just as hard for Sierra. Keep that in mind, okay?"

"Yeah, okay."

As Ben drove to Sierra's shop that evening, he was relieved the trial was over and in the hands of the jury. He didn't expect deliberation to take long, but he never really knew. There had been a couple of glitches and they might cost him. On the other hand, he'd presented the case to the best of his ability and he felt the facts were clear. The jury had to see that.

At Sierra's shop fifteen minutes later, he saw she had one clerk working with her. She looked up when he came in, her gaze questioning. But he just waited…waited for the customers to pay for their purchases and leave.

Finally, Sierra was finished at the register and no new customers had entered the shop. He went around the back of the counter, took her hand and tugged her into the workroom. She *did* look tired.

"What have you been doing to yourself this week?" he asked in a more curt tone than he should have. But he felt anger rising up that she wasn't taking care of herself.

"What do you mean, what am I doing? I'm running my shop."

"How long were you here yesterday?" he demanded.

She hesitated. "All day."

"And all evening?"

"I have two clerks sick. I had to step in and call Penny to help out when she could."

"What about the day before?"

"The same thing. Ben, what's this inquisition about?"

"Do you want to lose the baby? Is that what you're trying to do? If you didn't have this child to worry about, you could sell your shop and go to Africa if you wanted."

Her mouth rounded. Then she shut it and her cheeks took on more color. "I do *not* want to go to Africa. I do *not* want to lose this baby."

The fact that she was actually saying that she didn't want to leave cooled him down. But he was still worried about the long hours. "You *could* call a temp agency and get as much help as you need."

He'd never seen Sierra lose her temper. But now her dark eyes flashed, she squared her shoulders and she took a step back from him. "Ben, believe it or not, I ran my life just fine before I met you. I'm not taking any chances with my pregnancy. I make sure I'm not on my feet all day. I take breaks at least once an hour and put my feet up, even though the doctor says I'm perfectly fine. I had my appointment yesterday—Penny covered for me. If you'd called last night, you'd have known that."

"You could have called *me,*" he mumbled, feeling defensive.

"And interrupt the work that takes up all your focus for twenty hours a day? The work that's putting your life and mine in danger? The work that's depriving us from having a *real* marriage?"

"It's what I do!" he snapped, knowing she was right. "You knew when I married you what I did for a living."

"Yes, I did. But I never expected we'd live separate lives. This isn't just about us, Ben. You're worried about the baby? So am I. You said you want to be a full-time dad. How can you do that if you're never home? How can you do that if you only have limited time to give? How can we have any kind of relationship when all we do is have sex, then go our separate ways? I'm not sure why you're worried I'll go to Africa or why you even care. I want this baby to be more than a responsibility. *I* want to be more than a responsibility, more than a release for your stressful day."

There were tears in her eyes now as she concluded, "Maybe we should rethink our marriage. Maybe we should rethink what's really best for both of us and the baby."

Ben's past disappointments with women took over. As he did before, he wrapped himself in pride and let nothing show. "If that's what you want," he responded, his voice as even as he could make it.

The bell in Sierra's shop dinged and then dinged again. Ben knew he should say more. Do more. But at the moment he didn't know what that was. At the moment he was full of conflict and had to sort it all out. He did take his responsibilities seriously. But Sierra sounded as if that wasn't good enough for her.

He couldn't figure it out standing here, desiring her yet knowing their marriage was a mess. Knowing *he* was mostly to blame. "I'll let you get back to your customers."

"Ben—"

He held up his hand. "Maybe we both *do* have to rethink what we've gotten ourselves into. I'll call you this weekend, after we've both had time to think about it."

Then before the disappointment and yearning he was feeling got any worse, he left Sierra and her shop, headed for a house that used to be called home, but that now only seemed empty without Sierra in it. He had a bottle of tequila there that he'd never opened. Tonight he needed to empty his head. Then maybe tomorrow he could figure out what came next.

Sierra was in her shop on Friday afternoon and heard the news on the radio. The verdict was in—Charlie Levsin was guilty on all counts. She wanted to cheer, knowing what a victory this was for Ben. She also wanted to cheer because now it was all over.

Except…

She didn't know if she and Ben had a marriage. She didn't know if he *wanted* a marriage. She didn't know if he could ever trust her enough to believe in a marriage.

She'd spent last night crying because she never should have said they should rethink their marriage. Today she knew what she had to do. She loved Ben Barclay with all her heart and she had to tell him that, even if he didn't believe her. She had to tell him that no matter what, she was here for keeps. Eventually, maybe one day, he would believe he could count on her. He would believe she loved him. He would believe they were meant to be together.

Olivia had recovered from her illness and she was back today. She had two women covering the shop and that would just have to be enough, because she was going to track Ben down, throw her arms around him and convince him that this Christmas was going to be a happy one.

Fifteen minutes later, she stood in front of the building where the D.A.'s office was located. She stopped at the tall brick pillar with the eagle on top, studying it, absorbing what it meant. Freedom, maybe? There were all kinds of freedom, but freedom to love and believe in the future were the most important.

Dave stepped up beside her. "Maybe after today you won't need a chauffeur anymore."

"Tired of babysitting?" she joked.

"No, ma'am. I just meant that after today maybe you'd have your life back."

"I hope so," she confessed fervently. If she could see Ben, convince him that she loved him, everything would be fine, no matter what else happened.

Dave opened the glass door for her and they stepped inside the building. She hurried over to the receptionist's desk.

"I'm Mrs. Barclay," she said with a smile, taking out her driver's license for identification.

The receptionist checked Sierra's ID. "Mrs. Barclay! It's good to meet you. Congratulations on your marriage."

Sierra knew word traveled quickly in workplaces. "Thank you. Is Ben in his office?"

"No. In fact, you just missed him. He's probably in the parking lot. He had a meeting somewhere."

She and Dave had parked on the street. That's why they hadn't seen Ben. Now she tossed a thanks over her shoulder and, not waiting for Dave, hurried out the door and ran across the parking lot.

She spotted Ben at the far corner, behind his SUV. "Ben," she called.

He recognized her and she thought everything was going to be all right. She'd found him. She'd convince him she loved him. But then a man in torn jeans and a scruffy leather jacket appeared from the side of the car parked next to Ben's, and Sierra saw what he had in his hand—a gun.

She didn't think, not for a second. She just began running toward her husband.

"Sierra, don't!" Ben shouted because he'd seen the man, too.

She stopped, realizing she wasn't only putting herself in danger, but their baby, too. Yet she had to help the man she loved! She couldn't lose him. If only she could distract Levsin to give Ben a chance… She pointed behind Levsin and yelled the first name that came to her mind. "Over there," she shouted. "Miguel's coming."

As Levsin glanced over his shoulder, the man's momentary distraction gave Ben the opportunity he needed. Ready, his leg came up in some kind of martial arts move and he kicked at Levsin's midsection, apparently hoping to drop him to his knees. But although Levsin doubled over now because of the blow, he managed to hold on to his weapon. He aimed and fired.

"That's for my brother," he yelled as Dave appeared behind him and captured him in a choke hold until he released his gun. Another officer appeared from somewhere and helped, handcuffs ready.

Sierra ran to Ben's side, fell to her knees and saw the blood staining his white shirt. She couldn't lose him. She *couldn't* lose him.

Without thinking, she took off her own jacket and pressed it to the wound. "Hold on, Ben. Hold on." Tears came to her eyes and ran down her cheeks. The cold wind burned her face, but her gaze stayed on her husband's. "I love you, Ben. I love you. You can't die. You can't. Hold on."

All at once it seemed as if there were people everywhere—men in suits, police officers, bystanders. Then she heard the sirens and she prayed the ambulance would get here in time.

Ben tried to say something, but his eyes closed again and Sierra was afraid her love wasn't enough to keep him alive.

Ben's eyelids were so very, very heavy. He was swimming through some kind of fog, and his thoughts were slow in coming. They floated around him and he couldn't grasp them. Pictures came to him before words. All of them were pictures of Sierra—her beautiful face, her huge blue eyes, her wavy hair.

He saw her…then she was gone.

No! Don't go.

Had he ever told her not to go? Had he ever told her he wanted her to stay? Had he ever told her…

The image of her smiling face gave way to another. She was scared…so very scared. But even more determined than scared. He'd read that as she'd run toward him... *toward* him. He'd seen the moment she'd been aware of their baby's safety, too. Still, she'd found a way to help him. He'd been so reluctant to trust her. He'd tried to avoid disappointment...and hurt...and pain. But being separated from Sierra was painful. At that moment in the parking lot when he'd yelled for her not to get too close to him and she'd found a way that had saved them both, he'd known that he could trust her. Sierra was an unselfish woman who knew how to commit. He'd known she'd stay. He'd known he loved her in a way he'd never loved before.

He had to tell her so she'd know. He had to tell her so she wouldn't give up on him.

The fog sucked him back in again. The fog threatened to make him forget everything.

But he wouldn't. He loved Sierra. He would tell her as soon as he could make his lips move and his eyes open.

It was almost 2:00 a.m. when Sierra was allowed into Ben's room to sit by his bed until he awakened. His liver had been damaged, but he was going to be okay. He was going to live. The surgery had taken almost three hours and she'd held on to hope with both hands, praying every minute of that time.

Now she pulled her chair close beside him and took the hand that was free of the IV line into hers. She wasn't sure how long she sat there. The monitors beeped, nurses came and went and she held on to him, just as she was going to do for the rest of her life.

Finally, Ben's eyelids fluttered open and his gray gaze focused on hers. After licking dry lips, his voice was smoky and gruff as he managed to say, "You saved us. Why did you come to the D.A.'s office? Why were you there?"

She squeezed his hand tighter, saying the words overflowing her heart. "To see you. Because I love you and had to tell you. Because I should have told you a lot sooner. Because you're my husband and I intend to stand by you no matter what we have to face." Tears trickled down her cheeks.

Ben slipped his hand from hers and caught a tear with his thumb. "I've been such an idiot," he said, his voice gravelly and slow. "Do you know what you did out there today?"

"What?"

He took a deep breath, closed his eyes, then opened them again. "You made me realize what a fool I was, being afraid to trust you, being afraid to believe in us. I've been fighting hard against everything I feel. I've been calling it every name but what it was."

"What is it?" she whispered, her breath catching.

"I love you, Sierra Barclay." His voice was still hoarse, but it was strong. "Not because of the baby, not because of responsibility, not because anytime I'm with you I want to take you to bed. I've been afraid to let my guard down, afraid to feel anything for you. But I do. A whole world of feeling. I never guessed one person could mean so much to me. Have I ruined our chances by being blind and stubborn? Can you forgive me for doubting you?"

Sierra leaned close to him, rubbed her cheek against his, over his beard stubble. "I love you, Ben, and there's nothing to forgive. I should have gotten past my insecurities and told you I loved you sooner."

"You can tell me now, and every hour for the rest of our lives." Ben opened his arm to her. "Crawl in here with me."

She loved this man so. She'd almost lost him. She wouldn't deny him anything. Carefully, so as not to jostle him, she slid into bed beside him and laid her head on his shoulder. "What are we going to do when the nurses come in?"

"I'll tell them to go away or I'll have somebody arrest them."

She laughed, and it felt so good.

He added, "I'll also tell them that I need you by my side to recover. They'll understand. I love you so much, Sierra, that I'll spend every day proving it so you'll never doubt it. I promise you that. I promise you that I'm going to make some changes, and be a good husband and a good father."

She had no doubt that Ben would keep his word. He was a man of integrity and she would love him forever and beyond.

Ben's arm squeezed her tight against him as she lifted her lips for his kiss.

Epilogue

Sierra walked down the candlelit church aisle, looking like a princess. Ben wanted to run to her, scoop her up into his arms and carry her to the altar with him, where they were going to renew their vows. They were getting married all over again, with Sierra's parents, her aunt, *all* of his family witnessing the ceremony along with Camille and Miguel.

Sierra beamed at him as she took one step after another, still graceful, even six months pregnant. Her cream gown, with its long sleeves and empire waist, was beaded with tiny pearls. A lace mantilla was attached to a pearl headband that nestled in her dark brown hair. She wasn't looking anywhere but at him.

When she reached him, he took her hands, kissed first one and then the other.

"I'm so happy I could burst," she whispered in his ear.

"Thank you for loving me. Thank you for showing me each day how much I mean to you."

"You're my life, Sierra. You and the baby."

That fateful day in the parking lot, Ben had realized what true love was. He'd understood Sierra loved him and he loved her. Trust was part of the package.

Since then their lives had changed drastically. His recovery had taken six weeks. He and Sierra had done a lot of talking, a lot of thinking and a lot of dreaming during that time. He'd decided to resign as assistant district attorney and take the position as head counsel in the firm that would be helping first-time offenders. He saw it as a positive step, as a way to help kids turn in the right direction, as a way to keep them from ever stepping into the courtroom as defendants. Lois was the firm's PR person, but she was engaged now. He'd delegated another member of the team to work on public relations with her. Sierra had told him she trusted him and he believed her. But he also didn't want to give his wife any reason to be upset…any reason at all. She understood his work with kids and was a great sounding board when he wanted to bounce ideas around.

The priest's voice brought Ben back to the here and now as he began the ceremony, welcoming everyone. Corrie and Sam's baby gurgled and gave a little cry, as if she was delighted to be there. Sam's arm circled Corrie's shoulders as he gazed down at his child. Nathan, Kyle and Sara sat in the pew beside them, while Val and his dad, married now, looked on from behind. Sierra's parents and aunt were seated on the other side of the church. The two families had come together last night for dinner and had gotten along well. His dad admired the work Sierra's parents did. Her parents marveled at how he'd raised three sons alone. And her aunt Gina? Ever since she'd come to see him in the hospital after the shooting, she'd become more friendly. In fact, last night she'd given him a hug and thanked him for making Sierra so happy.

Ben's attention focused on his wife once more. He held her hand as they listened to the reading about unconditional love.

When the priest nodded to them to say their vows, Ben looked deeply into Sierra's eyes and spoke from his heart. "You are the love of my life. I can't imagine it without you. We started our journey a little differently from most, but I think that has given us even more of an appreciation for each other. I will always love you, care for you, respect you and take your needs into consideration, as well as our baby's. I will be the best husband and father I can possibly be. I will cherish each day with you, good or bad, praying we have at least seventy years to make each other happy. I love you, my darling, and I will never, *ever* take that love for granted."

Sierra's eyes were shiny with emotion as she smiled at him and then began her vows. "You are my home, Ben. I will go where you go and stand beside you every single day. You are my husband, my partner, my helpmate, but most of all, my best friend. I never had such a sense of belonging as I have with you. I feel safe, loved and oh so cherished. When our baby's born, I will do everything in my power to teach him or her to be a man or woman of integrity just as you are. I can't wait for our baby to be born. I promise to be the best mother I can learn to be. I love you, Ben, and for the rest of our lives I will be so grateful we found each other. I vow to make your goals and needs as important as mine, to always respect your beliefs, to understand your ups and downs and everything in between. I promise to love you forever."

Ben's throat was tight, his heart was beating hard, and he knew he'd remember this moment for as long as he lived.

After the priest spoke, then waited for them to exchange rings, Ben surprised Sierra with a diamond surrounded by turquoise in addition to her wedding band. When she saw it, she gasped and tears slipped down her cheeks. Ben wanted to surprise her again and again and see her radiant smile.

The ceremony seemed to be over in the blink of an eye. After the priest's blessing, Ben guided Sierra down the aisle, his arm around her. In the vestibule, he could no longer wait to kiss her.

With his lips melded to hers, their passion escalated as it always did. They'd be driving to a cabin near Taos for their honeymoon and he couldn't wait to get there. Sierra's hands were in his hair as he held her tight, kissed her deeper and longed for the union they experienced each time they made love.

Suddenly, there was the sound of applause and laughter. Ben heard his father's voice. "You'd better slow down or you're going to run out of steam."

He heard Nathan say to Sara, "Maybe we should renew our vows."

Sam cleared his throat loudly, then commented, "You're acting as if you haven't already been married for three months."

Still holding Sierra, Ben let his lips linger for a moment, then he broke their kiss and leaned away. "I can always count on my family to put in their two cents."

"Five cents," Sara suggested.

"Gotta keep up with the times," Corrie agreed.

Camille and Miguel hugged them, congratulating them along with the others.

Finally, Sierra turned toward her parents, her expression unsure, not knowing what to expect. However, her mother, father and aunt came toward her and Ben and hugged them both.

Sierra's mother, who looked very much like an older version of her daughter, gave Ben's arm a squeeze. "We didn't know what to think after she married you so fast. But over the past few months, we've seen how you love each other. Congratulations!"

Sierra's dad clasped Ben's shoulder. "We won't worry with you watching over her and the baby."

"Children grow up so fast," Sierra said. "I'll send you pictures, of course, but I hope you can really get to know your grandchild."

Sierra's mom smiled at her. "Your father and I have been talking about that. We've been offered positions at the university in the fall. We're seriously considering taking them."

Sierra's smile told Ben her happiness was complete.

"Okay, everybody," Camille said. "Time to celebrate. Let's go to the hotel and pretend that Ben and Sierra are newlyweds."

"We *are* newlyweds," they responded in unison, and everyone laughed.

Ben dipped his head to Sierra for one last kiss before they left. As his lips met hers, he murmured, "I think we've found our happily ever after."

Sierra's response assured him their happily ever after had only just begun.

* * * * *

Turn the page for a sneak preview of
AFTERSHOCK,
a new anthology featuring New York Times
bestselling author Sharon Sala.

Available October 2008.

nocturne™

Dramatic and sensual tales of
paranormal romance.

Chapter 1

October
New York City

Nicole Masters was sitting cross-legged on her sofa while a cold autumn rain peppered the windows of her fourth-floor apartment. She was poking at the ice cream in her bowl and trying not to be in a mood.

Six weeks ago, a simple trip to her neighborhood pharmacy had turned into a nightmare. She'd walked into the middle of a robbery. She never even saw the man who shot her in the head and left her for dead. She'd survived, but some of her senses had not. She was dealing with short-term memory loss and a tendency to stagger. Even though she'd been told the problems were most likely temporary, she waged a daily battle with depression.

Her parents had been killed in a car wreck when she was twenty-one. And except for a few friends—and most recently her boyfriend, Dominic Tucci, who lived in the apartment right above hers, she was alone. Her doctor kept reminding her that she should be grateful to be alive, and on one level she knew he was right. But he wasn't living in her shoes.

If she'd been anywhere else but at that pharmacy when the robbery happened, she wouldn't have died twice on the way to the hospital. Instead of being grateful that she'd survived, she couldn't stop thinking of what she'd lost.

But that wasn't the end of her troubles. On top of everything else, something strange was happening inside her head. She'd begun to hear odd things: sounds, not voices—at least, she didn't think it was voices. It was more like the distant noise of rapids—a rush of wind and water inside her head that, when it came, blocked out everything around her. It didn't happen often, but when it did, it was frightening, and it was driving her crazy.

The blank moments, which is what she called them, even had a rhythm. First there came that sound, then a cold sweat, then panic with no reason. Part of her feared it was the beginning of an emotional breakdown. And part of her feared it wasn't—that it was going to turn out to be a permanent souvenir of her resurrection.

Frustrated with herself and the situation as it stood, she upped the sound on the TV remote. But instead of *Wheel of Fortune,* an announcer broke in with a special bulletin.

"This just in. Police are on the scene of a kidnapping that occurred only hours ago at The Dakota. Molly Dane, the six-year-old daughter of one of Hollywood's blockbuster stars, Lyla Dane, was taken by force from the family apartment. At this time they have yet to receive a ransom demand. The housekeeper was seriously injured during the abduction, and is, at the present time, in surgery. Police are hoping to be able to talk to her once she regains consciousness. In the meantime, we are going now to a press conference with Lyla Dane."

Horrified, Nicole stilled as the cameras went live to where the actress was speaking before a bank of microphones. The shock and terror in Lyla Dane's voice were physically painful to watch. But even though Nicole kept upping the volume, the sound continued to fade.

Just when she was beginning to think something was wrong with her set, the broadcast suddenly switched from the Dane press conference to what appeared to be footage of the kidnapping, beginning with footage from inside the apartment.

When the front door suddenly flew back against the wall and four men rushed in, Nicole gasped. Horrified, she quickly realized that this must have been caught on a security camera inside the Dane apartment.

As Nicole continued to watch, a small Asian woman, who she guessed was the maid, rushed forward in an effort to keep them out. When one of the men hit her in the face with his gun, Nicole moaned. The violence was too reminiscent of what she'd lived through. Sick to her stomach, she fisted her hands against her belly, wishing it was over, but unable to tear her gaze away.

When the maid dropped to the carpet, the same man followed with a vicious kick to the little woman's midsection that lifted her off the floor.

"Oh, my God," Nicole said. When blood began to pool beneath the maid's head, she started to cry.

As the tape played on, the four men split up in different directions. The camera caught one running down a long marble hallway, then disappearing into a room. Moments later he reappeared, carrying a little girl, who Nicole assumed was Molly Dane. The child was wearing a pair of red pants and a white turtleneck sweater, and her hair was partially blocking her abductor's face as he carried her down the hall. She was kicking and screaming in his arms, and when he slapped her, it elicited an agonized scream that brought the other three running. Nicole watched in horror as one of them ran up and put his hand over Molly's face. Seconds later, she went limp.

One moment they were in the foyer, then they were gone.

Nicole jumped to her feet, then staggered drunkenly. The bowl of ice cream she'd absentmindedly placed in her lap shattered at her feet, splattering glass and melting ice cream everywhere.

The picture on the screen abruptly switched from the kidnapping to what Nicole assumed was a rerun of Lyla Dane's plea for her daughter's safe return, but she was numb.

Before she could think what to do next, the doorbell rang. Startled by the unexpected sound, she shakily swiped at the tears and took a step forward. She didn't feel the glass shards piercing her feet until she took the second step. At that point, sharp pains shot through her foot. She gasped, then looked down in confusion. Her legs looked as if she'd been running through mud, and she was standing in broken glass and ice cream, while a thin ribbon of blood seeped out from beneath her toes.

"Oh, no," Nicole mumbled, then stifled a second moan of pain.

The doorbell rang again. She shivered, then clutched her head in confusion.

"Just a minute!" she yelled, then tried to sidestep the rest of the debris as she hobbled to the door.

When she looked through the peephole in the door, she didn't know whether to be relieved or regretful.

It was Dominic, and as usual, she was a mess.

Nicole smiled a little self-consciously as she opened the door to let him in. "I just don't know what's happening to me. I think I'm losing my mind."

"Hey, don't talk about my woman like that."

Nicole rode the surge of delight his words brought. "So I'm still your woman?"

Dominic lowered his head.

Their lips met.

The kiss proceeded.

Slowly.

Thoroughly.

* * * * *

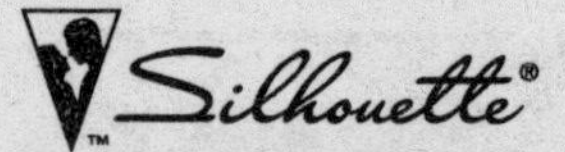

SPECIAL EDITION®

COMING NEXT MONTH

#1927 HAVING TANNER BRAVO'S BABY—Christine Rimmer
Bravo Family Ties
Tanner Bravo and Crystal Cerise had it bad for each other, though they couldn't be more different. Tanner was the type to settle down; free-spirited Crystal wouldn't hear of it. Now that Crystal was pregnant, would Tanner have his way after all?

#1928 FAMILY IN PROGRESS—Brenda Harlen
Back in Business
Restoring classic cars was widowed dad Steven Warren's stock in trade. And when magazine photographer Samara Kenzo showed up to snap his masterpieces, her focus was squarely on the handsome mechanic. But the closer they got, the more Steven's preteen daughter objected to this interloper....

#1929 HOMETOWN SWEETHEART—Victoria Pade
Northbridge Nuptials
When Wyatt Grayson's elderly grandmother showed up, disoriented and raving, in her hometown, it was social worker Neily Pratt to the rescue. And while her job was to determine if Wyatt was a fit guardian for his grandmother, Neily knew right away that she'd appoint him guardian of her own heart any day!

#1930 THE SINGLE DAD'S VIRGIN WIFE—Susan Crosby
Wives for Hire
Tricia McBride was in the mood for adventure, and that's just what she got when she agreed to homeschool Noah Falcon's two sets of twins. As she warmed to the charms of this single dad, Tricia realized that what started out strictly business was turning into pure pleasure....

#1931 ACCIDENTAL PRINCESS—Nancy Robards Thompson
Most little girls dream of being a princess—single mom Sophie Baldwin's world turned upside down when she found out she was one! As this social-worker-turned-sovereign rightfully claimed the throne of St. Michel, little did she know she was claiming the heart of St. Michel's Minister of Security, Philippe Lejardin, in the process.

#1932 FALLING FOR THE LONE WOLF—Crystal Green
The Suds Club
Her friends at the Suds Club Laundromat noticed that something was up with Jenny Hunter—especially Web consultant Liam McCree, who had designs on the businesswoman. Would serial-dating Jenny end up with this secret admirer? Or would a looming health crisis stand in their way? It would all come out in the wash....

SSECNM0908